City of Kaus
RESCUE

BOOK 3

DANI HOOTS

"While it is always best to believe in one's self, a little help from others can be a great blessing."

—Uncle Iroh

CHAPTER I

Cor

I downed the rest of my beer as I stared at the four Wanted posters. This was not good—there were probably men all over the city, looking for us. Was it because of the stuff that had happened on Zynon, or was it something else that Byron had put into place? Either way, it was a lot of money for whoever turned us in. Even I was tempted, not that they would give me the reward.

"We need to get out of here," Ellie whispered as if that was going to be a possibility.

Zach rubbed his face. He was tired. We were all tired. "Why can't we ever find a place to rest? I just want a nice, long bath and a cozy bed. I'm so tired of this shit."

I placed a couple of coins on the table for the bartender, and we turned to head out. Before we could get to the door, I heard the sound of a rifle cock. I sighed as we all raised our hands and turned back to the bartender. A rifle barrel was pointed straight at us.

"The poster says dead or alive, so unless you want to die here and now, keep your hands up while my waitress grabs your guns. I already alerted the authorities, so they should be here shortly."

We kept our hands up as a waitress with curly red hair and a green uniform took our guns and knives. Her hands were shaking, and she didn't meet any of our eyes. I wanted to comfort her and tell her not to worry, but there was no point. It wasn't as if she was going to believe some guy from a Wanted poster.

I knew we should have been more careful. I knew we should have headed straight out of town —although they would have stopped us at the border of the city. We should have been prepared. We should have known we weren't in the clear.

Once the waitress had finished grabbing our weapons, or at least visible weapons—I knew damn well that Ellie had more hidden away on her —the bartender gestured for us to sit down. We did as he asked.

"Hands on the table where I can see them." He never lowered his rifle.

"How about a drink while we wait then?" Ellie asked. "We're incredibly thirsty."

"I don't think so. You'll just wait here for the sheriff."

I raised an eyebrow. "Straight to the sheriff, eh? We must be really important. Any idea why they want us?"

"Like you don't know."

All four of us glanced at each other. If he only knew how long the list of things we could be wanted for really was. And I had a feeling it wasn't even for one of those crimes but something Byron had orchestrated.

"A reminder is always nice," Ellie commented with a fake cheery tone.

"Besides being Kausians, you murdered the mayor of this town and killed a lot of innocent people in the process. Blew up the neighborhood he lived in. There're a lot of people wanting you dead. You're lucky I'm not the murdering type. But I will pull the trigger if I need to."

When did Byron have enough time to pull that off? He literally had to have had that in place before he left Zynon and went to the Sirian Zone. Did he have a bunch of bombs and plans ready to go at his beck and call? What was this man capable of?

Zach rested his head on the table in defeat. There was no way we were going to be able to get out of this one. First the Silurians, then the Sirians, and now the humans were after us too. That only left the Lyrans, and who knew what Byron had set up over there?

Which meant we had only one direction to run—north into the mountains.

That is if we even made out of here alive. I had a feeling this could be the end of it all. It wasn't like there was anyone to save us. We didn't have friends —we didn't have a community. It was just the four of us, and we were all going to be arrested and possibly executed for our crimes or tortured by Byron just because he felt like teaching us a lesson.

Even if Byron only wanted me, he was going to take the others. He had a vendetta out for each of us, and I didn't think he was going to show us any mercy.

This was all my fault, and I knew it. If I hadn't decided I wanted to go to a university and just followed in my parents' footsteps, none of this would have happened. Because of me, my home was gone. Because of me, my friends were about to be arrested. Because of me, the entire world was in chaos.

I deserved to be captured, but not the others. They were innocent. They should make a break for it and leave me behind. Byron would take out all his frustrations on me—I knew that to be a fact. He liked messing with me—he liked to play with my head.

But would the three of them leave me behind? I wanted to say no—I wanted to say they would risk their lives for me, but I didn't know if that was the case. I didn't deserve their help. I didn't deserve anyone helping me. I was alone and I always had been. The more my secrets come out, the more I knew I didn't deserve friends who had my back. I was utterly alone, trying to pass the time until I met my end. Hopefully it was sooner rather than later. I didn't want to keep living like this.

The sheriff and his men took about ten minutes to arrive to the bar. I was watching the clock. It felt much longer—as if the second hand was moving through molasses. The bartender kept his rifle on us while the waitress helped any customers who came in and decided to stay even though there were wanted men in here.

No one seemed to pay us much mind, which was surprising. I expected people to either leave after what they had seen or, if they knew who we were, to throw punches and whatnot. The mayor in this town was quite popular. If only they knew the truth and would go after the person responsible.

The sheriff came with some of his officers. We must have been real popular. They searched each of us and found Ellie's other three weapons on her. I smiled a little. That was my Ellie—always ready for a fight. In this situation, however, we wouldn't get away and we all knew it. I had escaped a cell before and knew I would be able to do it again. I had a feeling Ellie and Zach also knew the inside of a cell as well as I did. Gabe, on the other hand, would have a steep learning curve.

I had to be honest though. I wanted to know what Byron's plan was. Had he known we would run away from the Sirian Zone? Was he going to set someone else up using the mayor's death and then decided on a change of plans? If that were the case, then who had he wanted to set up in the first place?

"The four of you are under arrest for the murder of Mayor Bartholomew Roberts," the sheriff, a dark-haired gentleman with a thick mustache and brown cowboy hat said as his men grabbed our wrists and cuffed us.

We didn't say anything as we knew there would be no point. Byron was good at planting evidence. How he was able to make it look like us, I had no idea. Half the things he can do seem impossible.

We were led outside and shoved into a police carriage. Bars made up all the sides and people were able to see us, yell at us, and throw things at us as we rode across town. It wouldn't be the first time I was in such a carriage, and it certainly wouldn't be the last.

"So what now?" Gabe asked as the carriage began to move.

I glanced over to Ellie and Zach. They both shrugged.

"We figure out a way to escape. Wouldn't be the first time we have broken out of prison," Ellie said.

Gabe's eyes lit up. "So you are able to break out of prison?"

She bit her lip. "Well, it depends on the prison. Some places are a lot less high-tech than others. In this area, it could go either way. Some prisons have both electric bars and mechanical ones, depending on the people they're holding."

"Except this time they think we killed a mayor, so I have a feeling it's going to be the electric one," Zach commented.

"What does that mean?" Gabe asked.

Ellie gave him a smile. "It means we'll have to think of a really good plan to escape."

She could say that again. Mechanical doors were pretty easy to pick. I was surprised they were still being used. Then again, you had to always have something to use for the pick on you when you were arrested, which wasn't always the case. I had a feeling Ellie did keep such tools on her person. The electric prisons, however, were impossible to unlock without a key, unless you didn't mind losing a hand. The best way to escape one of those was to wait until the door was opened by a guard and to overpower him without being shot. I had a feeling, though, they were going to have their guns on us anytime they came near the door.

We were royally screwed.

I stared down at the wooden carriage floor. Honestly, the best plan would be to try to escape at that moment. But with our hands tied like this, it would be near impossible. If it was just me, sure, I could get away. But with all four of us… Maybe if it was just Ellie and Zach, but with Gabe, it would be too hard. He didn't have street smarts like we did.

Then again, I could try to escape right now and save my own skin. The others could figure it out on their own. I fiddled with the cuff behind me. Anytime I could, I always put a piece of metal into my sleeve. With everything going on in the Sirian Zone, and since we had people after us, I was able to slip it in my sleeve before Byron captured me and tortured me. I passed out before I'd gotten the chance to use it.

So I could use it now if I wanted. I could make a break for it, and the others could do whatever they needed to escape. They were capable—Ellie and Zach would help Gabe, I was sure of that. One's own survival always took precedence—that was how I lived for the past three years. They knew that as well. Everything was easier if one was selfish.

And yet here I found myself in a group.

When had I become so soft? Why had I kept Gabe around? I should have let him go a long while ago. I had been on my own for a year, and I had been doing just fine in that time. Well, until the day Gabe found me stranded in the desert just south of where Kaus used to be. All the other trouble, however, I had to save his ass. So why didn't I let him go?

The carriage stopped. I had lost my chance to escape. I still had the piece of metal though, so when the chance was right, I could use it.

The officers pointed their guns at us as they unloaded and shoved the four of us into the building. People stared and watched as we were led toward the back of the building. And much to our dismay, Zach was right. It was an electric jail cell.

It would take a miracle for us to escape now.

CHAPTER II

Zach

Well, this certainly was a pickle.

I sat in the corner and leaned my head back on the wall. The stench of urine and sweat filled my nostrils. When was the last time this cell had been cleaned? I just hoped Byron would come and get us soon—I did not want to be in this cell any longer.

It was clear that this was Byron's doing. Who else would blow up the mayor and his surrounding neighbors just to pin it on someone else? There were a lot of horrible people in this world, but Byron was certainly taking the cake for the worst of the worst. I wasn't one to want someone to die a horrible death, but I wouldn't mind seeing Byron slowly killed in a public center. Hanging was always a fine choice.

I wasn't even sure how he was able to work so fast. I knew that question was on all our thoughts, even though it really wasn't that surprising. Byron had men everywhere we were finding out. He liked to play to dirty. It was a wonder that Gabe was still alive—it was a wonder how all of us were still alive. Then again, his plan worked and now we were stuck in prison—waiting for him to appear and haul us away, if we were lucky.

But for now, we were stuck here and there was no way that we were going to get out of this until they opened those doors and moved us to a different jail. Ellie and I had been in a lot of jail cells over the years, and the electric ones were always the worst. I had a few burn marks on my hands to prove it. It was better to wait and hope that someone would come for us soon.

Byron would know we would try to run, however, and would have a plan to keep us in check, just like he did for when we ran away from the Sirian Zone. We would have to be quick or outsmart him. We had done it before, so it was possible we could do it again. And again. And again.

Cor began pacing back and forth, glancing at the electric bars that kept us in there.

"What are you, a tiger or something?" I asked. "Keep your strength for when we bust out of here."

He rolled his eyes. "Moving around will keep my muscles warm. If you just sit until you need to escape, then you are going to strain something."

He had a point there. I brought my arm in front of me. "Here, I'll stretch. Does that work?"

Ellie let out a sigh. "Stop it, you two. Bickering isn't going to help us get out of here."

"You're just bitter because you would rather be making out somewhere."

I regretted saying it the moment it came out of my mouth. But I was hungry and tired, and I had a feeling none of us were making good decisions.

Gabe snapped to attention. "What?"

Yeah, this was a bad time to bring it up. I glanced away as both Cor and Ellie shot daggers at me.

"This isn't the time or place." Cor commented.

"Wait, so you two did kiss? When?" Gabe asked. "When?"

I kept my attention away from the three of them and stared at the walls. This was one interesting corner I found myself in. Oh look, a bug.

Cor answered Gabe. "Just when we were in the Sirian Zone. Look, it doesn't matter, okay? It's not something we need to deal with right now."

"So I don't matter?" Ellie bit back.

I glanced up. The ceiling was the same beige as the rest of the room. What were all those stains though? I tried not to think about it—I didn't want to know. I decided to turn back to the drama I kind of may have caused. Well, brought up. The three of them caused their own drama.

"That's not what I—" Cor began.

"Does anyone matter to you, Cor?" Ellie asked. "I mean, you didn't want to talk about it earlier, and you don't want to talk about it now. When will you sort all this out?"

Cor glanced at the both of them. Ellie crossed her arms. Cor shook his head. "We're in a jail cell. You all realize that, right? We could be sentenced to death soon if we don't get out of here. We need to take what energy we have left and start figuring out a way to escape."

Gabe shook his head. "You really can't talk about your feelings, can you?"

Cor rubbed his face. "Oh my goddess. Just… Look, I love you both, okay? I didn't believe I would find myself in this situation, so I haven't given it much thought. I don't want to lose either of you. So we need to focus on how to get out of this prison and find somewhere safe. Then we can talk this through."

"There is always something happening, Cor," Gabe said. "There isn't going to be any quiet time to figure this out. Not in our line of work."

Gabe had always seemed timid, but he was definitely speaking his mind now. I wasn't going to get in the middle of it all. No, I learned my lesson last time. I felt bad for all three of them. But they really needed to sort this out one way or another. I had a feeling, though, Cor was going to keep pushing the conversation back.

Cor shrugged. "Then it doesn't matter, does it? We'll all probably die anyway. It's not like we're going to all ride into the sunset and live a happy life. All of us are fucked."

It was quiet for a couple of minutes. Cor was right. We were completely fucked right now. However, that didn't mean they didn't need to work out what was going on between the three of them. Cor was just pushing away his problems, just as he normally did. We all had stuff we needed to work through, and it was clear that Cor needed to work on his fear of letting anyone in. But after everything that had happened, I couldn't blame him for just wanting to ride the good feelings as long as he could.

"Well." I finally broke the silence as it was more awkward than the arguing. "What should we do first? I don't know about you all, but I'm tired and hungry, and I don't believe they will be bringing us food any time soon."

Ellie sighed. "No, I don't think they will. But I also don't think we all should be asleep at the same time, just in case they try something dirty. I can take first watch."

"I'll stay awake too," Gabe said. "I'm not that tired."

I glanced over at the bunk bed. There were only two small cots anyway. There was no way all four of us were going to fit on it.

"I call top bunk," I commented. "Unless you really want to, Cor."

He let out a breath. "No, the bottom bunk is fine."

I climbed up on the top bunk and rested my head on the pillow. It didn't take long for unconsciousness to overwhelm me.

I woke to a voice.

It was Ellie and Gabe. They were whispering, but I was able to make out what they were saying.

"You don't happen to have a marker, do you?" Ellie asked.

"No, why?" Gabe asked.

"I was just thinking it would be a good idea to write on Cor's face while he slept."

Gabe chuckled. "He would be so mad. He cares about his looks a lot. Especially his hair."

"Of course he does. That's never changed."

There was silence for a moment. "What was he like when you were growing up?"

"He was sweet. Caring. Got into trouble a lot but usually for the right reasons. Usually. We would sneak out of Kaus since he had the codes to get back in if need be, but really we just ended up going through the main gate with some excuse or another. He never seemed to take anything seriously and kept a lot of secrets even from Zach and me, but his heart was always in the right place. I guess."

"So not too much has changed," Gabe commented. "You two have been through a lot then."

"I suppose so. Kaus wasn't the greatest place to live, but at least we had a community. Everyone watched each other's back. Well, for the most part."

"Except for half-Kausians?"

Ellie hesitated. "Yeah. Zach was bullied a lot, and many of the adults didn't treat him well. But we were there for him—both Cor and me. So when Cor left… we just couldn't believe it."

"Because you two were madly in love."

Ellie was silent for a moment. That was true— they were madly in love. It was a love that I knew I could never be a part of. I was happy for them— they were perfect for each other. But every time I thought about the future, I feared I wouldn't be in it and that they would leave me behind. It ate at me every day. Then, after everything that had happened, it was just Ellie and me, and I was happy. Except I knew it shouldn't be like that. I knew Ellie's heart had been broken and that the two of them should have lived happily ever after. I just didn't want to be alone.

So now that Cor was back in the picture, I didn't know how to handle it. I wanted to be angry at him, but none of this was his fault. I needed to deal with my emotions—I needed to tell Ellie how I felt about being her best friend and not wanting that to change. I didn't want to be her boyfriend or anything like that, but I didn't want to lose the friendship we had.

"We were in love," Ellie said. "But I don't know what it is now. I care about him, but all of this… Well, it's all fucked up. I'm sorry you got dragged into this. I'm sorry… I kissed him."

I wondered if Cor was awake like I was or if he was still sleeping. I hoped he could hear what they were saying. Maybe he would man up and finally tell them how he felt. The odds were slim though.

"I'm not mad at you. I'm just… It's barely been a week, and my whole world has been flipped upside down practically. It's a lot to process. We'll figure it out in the end. Or at least I hope we make it through to the end."

Neither of them said anything because, well, it was true. We didn't know if we were going to get out of this or if we were going to make it out of here alive. I took a few long breaths and tried to fall back asleep. I had a feeling the next day was going to bring much more chaos, and we had to be ready. After a few moments, I was out like a light.

CHAPTER III

Gabe

I wasn't sure if Cor heard what Ellie and I had discussed while we were awake, but he didn't act like he had heard anything. He was either asleep through it all or was very good at hiding his thoughts and emotions. Problem was, I knew he was good at hiding his emotions, so it was hard to tell. He was a good actor and if the cards were different, he could have gone to school for acting.

I wasn't going to get anything out of him, and I knew that. And I would have to accept that.

At least for now. I understood he didn't want to deal with more stuff when our lives were literally at stake. But this would need to be sorted in the end, one way or another. And if we died, then it didn't matter. Which, I had a feeling, was what he was counting on in a way. I really didn't want to die and yet, here we were, in prison awaiting my uncle who was probably going to kill us. I just wanted to live my life, was that to much to ask?

I supposed the other three felt the same. If my uncle hadn't decided to destroy Kaus, then Cor and Ellie would still be together, and probably married. Eventually they would have a kid, and I wouldn't have been a part of their lives.

That was the wosrt part of it all. Cor and Ellie had grown up together—they had been engaged. There was never a real break-up for them, and they always loved each other. It was Cor who had tried to run away from everything and thought that she would never love him again. He had been wrong.

So what if Cor told Zach and Ellie the truth of

what happened right away? Would we have never met? Would we have never fallen in love? Was I the expendable one here?

I curled into a ball on the bunk. There was no way I was going to fall back asleep at this rate. All my memories of growing up came rushing back to me. I had always been abandoned. My father abandoned me. My country abandoned me. My uncle turned everyone against me. The only person who did care about me was my mother and Krisian and both of them were dead. I was truly alone, and I thought for once in my life that I had someone who needed me—who wanted me—and I had been wrong. Cor didn't need me—not in the way I needed him. I was just a means to an end. He hadn't thought that far ahead—he was never picturing a future with me. I should have known better. I should have known he would leave me too.

Shutting my eyes as tight as I could, I tried to push back those thoughts. He hadn't left me. He wasn't going to leave me. These people were my family now. Just because I wasn't one of them didn't mean they would leave me. They had protected me in the Sirian Zone. They wouldn't abandon me now. Not after everything.

But was it because they wanted to help me or was it because I had the money to keep them alive? Did they just want to use me for funds? No, they knew that once my people attacked me that I would be cut off from any accounts. Or at least I figured I was. I could try to access them, but the odds were that it would alert anyone to my location. Money was the least of our worries now, however, since we were, well, in jail.

What was Byron's plan? What did he want from us now?

He could have ordered us dead on the spot, but he didn't. It was more than likely he wanted to watch us die, but that would give use the chance to get away. Did he like the chase? Did he like trying to pin us down so that we felt inferior? Odds were, that was what it was. He always tried his hardest to make me feel little.

I took a few breaths to compose myself before getting up. I knew I had only slept a couple of hours, but I doubted I was going to get any more sleep. I mind as well do something productive, if that was even possible in a jail cell.

I found Zach and Cor sitting on the ground with their backs against the wall. They didn't really pay much mind to each other. It seemed the two of them had their own issues to sort through as well. It was a shame, as I could tell they used to be the best of friends.

A friendship I never would understand.

I pushed back those feelings of loneliness that kept surfacing to the top. They wouldn't be of any help. Just because I didn't have childhood friends didn't mean I had to that ping of hatred for others who did have that type of relationship.

"Awake already?" Cor asked.

I nodded. "Yeah, can't sleep. Too much going on."

"You can say that again." Ellie groaned as she rolled over. Apparently she couldn't sleep either.

Jumping off the top bunk, I glanced out of the electric bars that held us in. Behind the bars, there were a couple of guards. We were always been watched. There was no way we would be sneaking out of here. We would have to fight.

Ellie sat on the ground, and I took a seat beside her. She leaned in, glancing at the guards. "So, how is this going to go down?"

Cor shrugged. "Unless they come to take us somewhere, I don't see us getting out of here anytime soon."

Zach added, "Byron won't take long to wrap up in the Sirian Zone—he will come for us."

I commented, "It won't take him long to convince the Sirians that I'm to be hunted and killed and that they should listen to him to get the zone back to normal. They'll close off everything."

"Which means they won't do anything if a war breaks out on land." Cor let out a sigh. "He really does have all this planned out, doesn't he?"

We all nodded.

"So that just leaves a plan for how we're going to get out of this. Zach and I have broken out of plenty of jail cells, but the electric ones are always the worst. If the guards come, I'm sure Byron will warn them or has already warned them we'll try something," Ellie said.

"What if we fake an illness or something?" I asked. "I mean, that always seems to work in the books I've read."

The three of them chuckled. Ellie answered, "Yeah, that doesn't work. It depends on the situation, sure—it could work—but when you are wanted like we are, it won't work. They don't care if we live. I'm not even sure if we're going to be given any food or water until Byron gets here."

My stomach growled at the mention of food. I was definitely hungry and wanted something to eat, not to mention I really needed a drink of water. I was starting to get a headache from dehydration.

"Then what can we do?" I felt helpless at that point. Was there any way to get out of this, or were we sitting ducks? And once Byron was there, was he going to keep us alive? I had a feeling, in my case, he would throw me back to my people who would more than likely sentence me to death, which I couldn't blame them. It really did appear as if I had killed my mother.

I still couldn't believe she was gone. I wasn't sure if I had processed any of it. She was going to tell the world of what crimes Byron had committed —she had been our last chance. Now she was gone. I would never hear her voice again. I would never be comforted by her again.

I felt tears begin to trickle down my face. I glanced up to find everyone staring at me. I didn't want to cry in front of them, but now that I had a moment to think about everything that happened, all my emotions came pouring out.

Cor was the first to move over to me and wrap his arm around my shoulder. "It's all right. We'll get out of this."

I shook my head. "It's not that. Well, it is, partially. But just… My mother is gone. My sister is all alone. And Krisian sacrificed himself to save me. I just… I don't know what to do anymore."

Ellie and Zach moved closer and put their hands on me.

Ellie commented, "I know it's a lot. But you'll make it through. We'll get revenge for all the lives that have been lost. You are not alone in this. We'll make him pay."

Zach added, "And once the truth is out there, we

can get your people to understand what happened and go help your sister."

I wanted to tell him that wasn't going to happen. Even once everything was out in the open, I doubted my people would let me come back. I still had killed soldiers. They still didn't like what I was —half human and not one of them. Perhaps I could see my sister, but I would not be welcomed.

"Thank you, everyone. It means a lot to have you here with me. I haven't ever had anyone in my life to comfort me like this—to listen to my concerns and not tell me it's in my head."

But how long would that last? I felt as if it were fake. I felt that once this was over, I would lose everything. They would move on without me, wouldn't they? No, I needed to stop thinking that. They wouldn't leave me behind. If they wanted to, they could have escaped the Sirian Zone without me, but they didn't. They were my friends. I had to remember that.

And they would be there when we got out of here. We would stop Byron together.

CHAPTER IV

Ellie

Byron had destroyed so many lives.

If someone had told me this was all due to one man, I wouldn't have believed them. But it had been—all of this was truly due one crazed individual with too much power. He was able to persuade people, just as his father and grandfather did. But it was time for him to be stopped.

And we were the only ones who could stop him.

I presumed there were others—at least a few people who were against him and were trying to take him out. There had to be, right? The entire population couldn't be convinced he was doing this for the greater good, could they? Gabe's friend had helped us—that meant there had to be more that would help us. The problem was, how did we find them, and how did we get them to help some Kausians?

Even if it wasn't everyone who sided with Byron, most people probably just kept their heads down and didn't say anything. As far as I was concerned, not standing up to him was the same as siding with him. He wanted genocide, and there was no excuse for staying silent. Even if it cost us our lives, we had to do something.

Otherwise, there would be no world to come back to.

My conclusion was that no one believed it would affect them—or perhaps they didn't things could get as bad as it was most likely getting. I'm sure the Silurian Krax never saw it coming. The two of them had been partners until Byron betrayed him. I could only imagine the betrayal Krax felt when Byron's men tried to capture him while Zach was forced to transform like him and order Krax's men to open fire on the poker tournament. Krax was able to put two and two together, and knew Byron was trying to start a war just before Byron shot him.

It made sense that Byron went after the Silurians first since they were the biggest threat besides us Kausians. According to Byron, the Kausians used to be a populous and well-accepted society. Many of the other races even feared us. But then Byron's grandfather sowed the seeds of mistrust and made our people outcasts. Shifting became illegal, and we all hid in our zone.

The only reason I believed that story to be true was because of the defense technology we had. It was expensive, and there would be no way that we would have been able to install it unless we were once a rich nation. The shield also expanded farther into the desert than the boundary of the town. Growing up, I had always wondered why. Now I knew the truth.

Although we had books and such, a lot of our history books had been destroyed. I wasn't sure what the entire story with that was, but I had a feeling Byron's family had something to do with it. Knowledge was one of the strongest weapons after all and if you took that away, you could convince anyone of lies.

I bit at my fingernail as I paced back and forth in the cell. So far there had been no word from Byron or the guards. Sure, they gave us a little food and water, which was surprising, but they had slid it under the electric bars so we weren't able to ambush them. There was also not much food on the plates and all of us were still hungry. It was a way they were trying to keep us week. Unfortunately for them, us Kausians were used to not getting enough to eat and knew how to push past that feeling.

"You are going to waste all your energy," Cor commented in a sarcastic tone. It was what Zach had said to him just hours before. I shot him a look and kept moving.

"We need to get out of here, and I'm not sure how," I sighed.

"Maybe if you go back and forth enough times, you will wear a hole in the ground and we can crawl out of here."

I rolled my eyes. Digging was never a good option. I would know and so would he.

Zach grabbed the hem of my shirt and pulled me down to sit.

I let out a breath as I folded my arms in front of me. "Sitting isn't going to help."

"Shh," he whispered. "I think I have an idea."

Gabe and Cor gathered around him, and he kept his voice hushed, glancing at the guards to make sure they didn't hear us. "Look, the guards having been discussing something and looking over at us. I think they are going to move us soon or they are expecting Byron to come soon."

We all glanced over. It did seem like they were getting ready for something or someone. Earlier they had been just playing cards and taking about random things.

"So are we going to rush them?" I asked. "Or are we going to wait until we're on the road again?"

"What if he doesn't want us moved? What if he

just comes to kills us?" Gabe asked.

We were all silent for a moment. He had a point. Byron probably just wanted us out of his hair. He didn't want to have to deal with our kind anymore.

Cor shook his head. "No, he wants to wait until all this is over before he kills us. He wants to rub it in our face that we failed to stop him. And then he will shoot us or stab us. I feel like he's more of a gun man."

That was another good point. I let out a huff as I rubbed my face. How did we get stuck in such a shitty era? This was not fair. I just wanted to live my life with the ones I loved. Was that too much to ask? I didn't even care if it was within a town or not. I'd be happy in the middle of nowhere with my own little farm.

Zach and I had tried that, however, and it didn't end well. Bandits had attacked us a few times before we decided we couldn't live in the wilderness. They were constantly on the lookout for people to steal from, whether it was by tracks or smoke from a fire. Bandits were always searching and one was never safe. At least, in the more habitable areas. The desert and mountains were clear of them, but those areas were so harshed, it wasn't worth it. At least, unless it was a last-minute situation.

"So we fight and pray that we don't get shot. Is that the plan?" I asked.

"Isn't that always the plan?" Cor half grinned.

Wasn't that the truth? I scratched my scalp, my salt-crusted and oily hair feeling disgusting even though I was used to it. I always wanted to just cut all my hair off, but Cor had always loved my hair, so I kept it long. Even after all this time.

"What if we get separated? Where should our meet-up location be?" Gabe asked.

Zach rubbed his beard. "Well, we aren't exactly welcomed in this city or any other city, so it will have to be somewhere no one expects us or recognizes us."

"Which leaves nowhere." I sighed. "Maybe outside the city?"

"The guards will be looking for us," Cor pointed out. "So we would have to sneak out of here, which is going to be difficult."

We were silent for a moment. We really had nowhere to go—at least, not in the city. If we could get outside the border, then we could hide somewhere even though there were bandits. With four of us, we could take them on. And we could head north where there weren't any bandits. The snow was deep, and it would be hard to get by, but we wouldn't have to worry about anyone finding us.

But we couldn't exactly meet all the way out there. First off, it was to many square miles to try and locate someone, even if we tried to use landmarks. Then there was the fact that if the other person didn't show, we would have no idea where to start looking.

"There are a couple of not-so-great bars underground. Lot of criminals hang out there. At least the people working the bar would let us in, no questions asked. We still run the risk of one of the other people at the bar turning us in, but they don't like to deal with officers either, so it should be okay. Gabe will just have to stay close to us," Cor explained.

"That doesn't narrow it down. Which bar are you talking about?" I asked.

"The Royal Straight," Cor said.

Zach and I glanced at each other. He was right. No one there would turn us in. We had gone to that bar a couple of times for clients. It was dangerous, but so was staying in this prison.

"All right," I said. "That is where we'll meet if we manage to escape and get separated."

"And what if one of us doesn't escape at all?" Gabe asked. "Do we leave them?"

I glanced at Zach. We had always made a pact that if there was no way to safely rescue the other person, then we would leave them. It had never come to that, however, but the pact was still there.

"We do what we need to to survive." I took a breath. "And take down Byron."

CHAPTER V

Cor

So this was going to end up horribly.

Not that was any different from normal. It seemed like we were always getting the short end of the stick nowadays. With Krax dead, that should have been the end of it. I could never have imagined what more was planned out after the destruction of Kaus. If only I hadn't been deceived by Byron and realized he was the mastermind behind it all. Perhaps things would have ended differently.

I just hoped none of us got stuck in the shootout that our plan was going to cause. There were pros and cons to there being four of us. The pros were that we more than likely outnumbered the guards that would be transporting us. The cons were that we were less sneaky and made up more area for guards to shoot at.

Ellie had said that we would do what we needed to survive. I would never have expected her to say that—especially when it came to Zach. I had assumed they would always die for each other—use whatever means they could to save each other. Perhaps I was wrong. Perhaps they would have left the other to rot in jail if there was no way to save them without risking their own life.

Or she was just saying that in case Gabe or I got left behind. That seemed more likely. She wouldn't come back for me, and neither would Zach. That was no surprise—I had destroyed our entire lives after all. And yet, for some reason, that stung a little. There was a time in our lives that would do anything for each other. Was that feeling gone? Or was that just the way of our lives now?

After we discussed where to meet up, we talked about how we would distract the guards and get out of there. Between all of us, we were able to figure out the layout of the entire building. Zach, Ellie, and I had gotten into the habit of planning escapes and noting where all the doors and windows were when officers led us to a cell. Gabe, of course, had not. When this was over, we would definitely need to start teaching him different tactics on how to stay alive. I had no idea how he was able to survive before he met me. Luck, I supposed. Luck that would have eventually run out.

I worried that we wouldn't be able to make it out, and Byron would finally have us in his custody. I knew he wouldn't kill us outright; however, that didn't mean he wouldn't torture us. He would make us watch as he hurt the others, and I didn't know if I could stand that. It was hard enough having the Kausian beat me until I passed out—what if he had more Kausians? What if he told them Ellie and Zach were also responsible for what happened?

Shaking my head, I pushed away those thoughts. If I spent too much time worrying about what-ifs like that, I wouldn't be able to focus on escaping. If those things came to pass, then I could figure out how to solve them. Odds were they weren't going to happen, but I couldn't help but have a nagging feeling that things were going to take a weird, random turn for the worst.

I mainly had that feeling because there were many things that could go wrong with the plan we had set up—mainly because we were going up against Byron and he always seemed to be one step ahead of us. It was a miracle we hadn't been killed by him yet, and as the miraculous escapes increased in number, I had a feeling he would care less and less about making us watch his horrible master plan take effect. He already had so many species against each other, and even if he stopped now, there would be a lot to clean up. The decades of racism that were already interwoven into the society would take even longer to come undone.

So what were we even doing? Why did we want to stop him? People were simply destroying themselves by believing lies. There were many people in the world who could stop him—who could stand up to him—but they simply didn't. Or at least it seemed that way.

It felt as if we were the only ones up against the world.

To be honest, we were doing this for selfish reasons. We wanted revenge on the life he took away from us—revenge for all the lives he murdered in Kaus. We wanted to see him suffer and feel what we felt.

As I pondered on those thoughts, I noticed a few more guards come into the room between our cell and the hallway. They spoke to each other. I glanced at the others. We all nodded.

This was it. They were going to try to move us. It was our chance to escape. Or get killed in the process. It could go either way.

I was still weak from everything that had happened in the Sirian Zone, not to mention covered in bruises, and wanted more than anything to just curl up into a ball and sleep—but I knew that wasn't going to happen. I was running on adrenaline now—adrenaline that keep me alive.

The four guards came up to the cell—all humans —and they had their guns pointing at us. One of them barked out, "Hands on the wall! Now!"

We turned and did what they asked. If we were going to get out of there, we would have to be quick.

As we placed our hands on the walls, three of the guards put their guns away and pulled out handcuffs. The fourth guard kept his gun level.

It was still better than all four guns on us.

As the door opened and the guards stepped inside the cell, Ellie, Zach, and I glanced at each other. This was it. We were going to overtake them.

One of the guards stepped up behind me and tried to grab my arms to bind them in the handcuffs. Instead, I swung my head back and headbutted him straight in the forehead. It wasn't enough to make him fall but enough for him to lose his balance and need to gather himself. I spun around and tackled him to the ground, grappling with him to get his gun.

Ellie and Zach attacked with similar force and

style, making the guard with the gun hesitate and not know where to shoot first. Before he could make a decision, I shot him in the chest. It was clear the guns were filled with stun bullets as there was no blood.

The guard I struggled with tried to take the gun back, and I used the butt of it to knock him out. Ellie and Zach were able to get the guns from the other guards and knock them out. The three of us stood up as Gabe stared at us.

"I definitely have more to work on, don't I?" Gabe asked.

I ruffled his hair. "Don't worry. We'll train you soon. But for now, just stay low and out of sight."

"The guns are filled with tranks," Zach commented. "The signs may have said they wanted us dead or alive, but it's clear that the guards were ordered to take us in alive."

I nodded. "Yeah, I was equally surprised. But that doesn't mean they won't try to kill us when we escape. Gabe, grab the other gun and don't hesitate to shoot."

Gabe did as I asked of him. He didn't have the

best aim, but at least he had something. I had a feeling his aim was always off because deep down he didn't want to hurt anyone. This way, he didn't need to worry about that.

We stepped out into the guards' room and slowly opened the door to the hallway. Ellie and Zach grabbed our bags that they had taken from us when we came in, which included Ellie's favorite gun and some cash. We would definitely need that.

I peered out and watched as guards came flooding toward us. They must have heard the gunshots. I began to shoot at them, hoping that the gun had a full round of bullets.

I was able to take two down with just two shots and Ellie and Zach helped me knock out five more. We waited a moment, listening for any noise in the quiet that surrounded us. When we came in, I noted at least a dozen guards. So far we had taken down eleven.

Was that all of them? We were in the clear. I motioned to the other three to cover me as I went out and checked.

That was one of the worst mistakes I had made in

the past couple of weeks. I felt the bullet hit me straight in the leg. A real bullet—not a trank.

"Shit!" I cursed as I hit the ground. Before the guard could rush me or shoot the others, Ellie got him with the trank.

The three of them tried to rush to my side, but it was too late. Three more guards appeared and started to open fire with real guns. I kept down on the ground with my arms raised.

I glanced back to find Ellie, Zach, and Gabe running out the back door they had found. I tried to stand to get to them, but the guards shouted at me.

"Stay down or we'll shoot! Hands up in the air! Kick your gun to us!"

I did as they asked, my eyes making contact with Ellie's for one brief second before they left me there. I took a deep breath and let it out slowly.

They had left me to save their own skin. Just like we promised.

The guards came up to me, guns pointed down. One took the gun I had slid away, and the other slammed me to the ground and wrenched my arms behind my back to bind my wrists. Before they pulled me back up, I heard a voice above me.

"Well, well. Looks like someone's friends abandoned him."

I glanced up to find Byron smiling. He nodded to the guards.

"Throw him in the carriage."

"What about the others, sir?" a guard asked.

"Don't worry about them. I'll deal with them later."

Byron bent down and grabbed my chin—forcing me to look at him. "I don't believe the two of us finished our conversation."

"I have nothing to say to you."

He laughed as he stood up. "Let us leave. I have a lot I need to finish before I head to the Lyran Zone."

With that, the guards hauled me up and took me out toward his carriage.

CHAPTER VI

Zach

"We have to go back for him!" Ellie exclaimed after we ran for at least five minutes, twisting and turning through alleyways until we didn't see any guards follow us. I glanced around and found that we were in an area that was probably not much safer than the cell we had left.

I watched as two hooded figures entered one of the buildings, their bloodshot eyes surveillaning us for a moment, making sure we weren't going to follow them. I did not want to know what was happening beyond those doors, but if I had to guess, it was probably something to do with drugs. I couldn't blame them for wanting an escape from this world. I knew I wanted to run away as well.

"We can't, Ellie. We made a promise that we would save our own skin before anyone else's. Or did you forget that promise?"

She shook her head. "I didn't think any of us would actually fall behind. Besides, if I was the one captured, can you honestly say you wouldn't have returned for me?"

I frowned. She was right. We had made the pact, but both of us knew we wouldn't have followed it. As for Cor, however, I knew he wouldn't have come back to save any of us. He would have run and kept on running. That was what he did all those years ago and that's what he would have done today "I may not have followed our pact, but can you honestly say Cor would go back for you? For any of us"

Ellie didn't say anything but turned her head. She

knew I was right.

Gabe intervened. "He would. He's gone back for me several times since we have been together."

"No offense, Gabe," I began. "But that's because you had money. He's left the two us behind before, and I don't doubt that he wouldn't do it again."

Gabe appeared a little surprised I had been that straightforward with him, but then he shook his head. "He didn't know how much money I had back then. I never told him the truth of who I was until a few days ago when I told you two as well. Sure, together we were able to earn a lot, but I wasn't his main source of income. He cares more than he lets on. He's just… bad at showing it or saying it."

We were silent for a moment. Cor not being able to express his emotions was quite the understatement. He had both Ellie and Gabe wrapped around his little finger and wasn't going to straighten any of that out if he could help it. They weren't thinking clearly—they were blinded to the fact that if we tried to save him, we would be captured or killed. Cor could make it out on his own far better than if we tried anything. We needed to just head to where we planned and hope for the best.

I rubbed my beard. "I just… It's hard after so many years to think he has changed—especially since he left us. Besides, we don't know where he will be taken. It was clear Byron was there and has retrieved him. There's also the fact he's injured, so it's not going to be an easy retrieval mission."

"We could head back and see where the carriage is going," Ellie said. "But that will mean the guards might see us."

Gabe replied, "I think I know where he's taking him. He has a house in the next town over—an estate really. It's huge, and he has his own guards and many places where he could lock up Cor. I assume he'll be staying there as he sets his next plan in motion."

"Oh, this keeps getting better." I let out a sigh. "Let me guess—countless guards, a high-tech security system, lots of guns, lots of locked doors, and so forth?"

Gabe nodded. "Yup. Exactly that."

"Well." Ellie clapped her hands. "At least we know where he is. And we know Byron probably won't be looking for us that hard since he believes we're stupid enough to follow him. Should we find some food, get our horses, and take camp somewhere outside the city?"

I rubbed my face. Those were all things I definitely didn't want to do. Well, except for the food part. I was starving.

"Fine. Let's get some food. But we'll have to hire some kid to retrieve it for us. I have a feeling our faces are still plastered everywhere."

"Which is going to make getting our horses back a little difficult." Ellie held up her gun. "But I think I'm pretty persuasive when I need to be."

I knew the food was probably bland and nothing fancy since it was a pasty from a street vendor, but after a day of no food it was the most magnificent thing I had ever had. It was simple, easy to eat, and easy for the kid we hired to go fetch it for us. Mine was filled with mashed potatoes, beef, gravy, and some vegetables. It was delightful. Luckily, we'd grabbed our bags on the way out of the jail and had some money still in them. Ellie and I learned that simple thing was very, very important to do when you were running away from law enforcers. You only make that mistake once.

So we had some money, and we had our weapons. Ellie would have definitely gone back to get her gun Crazy Jack if we had left it. It was her favorite weapon and had a special place in her heart. Although I liked my own weapon, Lucky Susan, I wouldn't have risked my life to go back for it. She would have and to this day I still wasn't sure why she loved it so much.

Charlotte Hunkerbink III, however, I would risk my life for, and technically we were. There was no way the man was just going to give us back our horses—not with how many Wanted posters there were. We were even risking our lives having the kid get us food since he could have seen the posters as well. Luckily the kid wanted the money we were giving him, or he hadn't paid much attention to any posters around town.

We kept our heads down as we ventured through

the city toward where we were keeping our horses. I was glad Ellie remembered where they were because I was completely turned around. Although we had spent a few months at a time in this city, that didn't mean I was completely used to this place. All the towns and cities started to mush together in my mind, and I easily got turned around.

We made it to the stalls, and Ellie didn't even hesitate to pull out her gun. There was no one else there but the owner and a couple of workers, thank goodness.

"Hands up! We're getting our horses and leaving this place. As long as you don't move a muscle, we won't have any trouble, now will we?"

The man's eyes were wide. "You three… You are the ones on the Wanted posters."

"Right, which is why we're getting our horses and leaving this place. I already paid you for their time here, so no one is going to lose in this transaction—as long as you stay right there." She nodded to the two workers. "And you two—stay where I can see you. If you value your lives."

Her gun was full of tranks, but they didn't know that. They just saw three desperate criminals trying to get their horses so they could escape the city.

The old man glanced around with his glossy eyes but didn't say anything. He clearly had no way to fight back, and the guards were nowhere near this establishment. The workers kept still, not wanting to get in the middle of this and not paid enough to really help their boss.

Ellie motioned the gun toward the back of the stables. "Zach, go get the horses. Gabe, help him."

Gabe followed me to where our horses were being kept. Both of them neighed as they saw me. I opened the stall doors and patted them.

"How have you two been? Were you good horses? Of course you were! Did they treat you well?"

Char nodded and stamped her hoof on the ground. Kevin huffed, which meant he was happy as well. He wasn't as cheerful as Char. They matched Ellie's and my personalities and I loved that most about them. I grabbed the saddles and placed them on each of the horses. Gabe helped me tighten them. It was clear this wasn't the first horse he had ever ridden, which I was glad. It wasn't easy to teach others to ride a horse when you were running for your life.

We corralled the horses to the front of the stable where Ellie was holding the workers hostage. As we entered, she rummaged through her bag and tossed the workers a couple of coins.

"Here, since I know he's probably not paying you enough for this shit."

With that, Ellie swung up on Kevin and helped Gabe up behind her since both of them were rather small and I was a bit larger. I climbed up onto Char.

Ellie snapped the reins, and we got out of there as quickly as we could. Now the hardest part would be getting through the border that led out of the city.

We made it a few blocks, checking behind us to make sure the owner of the stall didn't call on any officers after we left. There wouldn't have been any point since he didn't have us cornered. They weren't going to give that award out unless the person actually captured us. Ellie led us into an alleyway, and we turned to face each other and talk.

"Gabe, how well can you ride a horse?" she asked as she turned her head to see him.

He shrugged. "All right. I mean, I didn't grow up with the creatures of course, but I have ridden a few over the years."

I knew what she was going to suggest. "You can't be serious."

"It's the only way to get through the border. I'm going to make a diversion, leading the guards away, and then when you rush them, I'll jump on one of your backs, and we'll make our great escape."

"You know that's the worse plan you have come up with, right?" I asked.

She shook her head. "Honestly, it's not the worst. Will it work? Well, we shall see. It's our only shot at getting out of here alive."

Ellie had a point there. "Well then, let's get on with it."

CHAPTER VII

Gabe

I didn't know what to think about this.

First off, although I could ride a horse, I wasn't sure if I could ride a galloping horse with people trying to stop me. More often than not, Cor and I took trains to get around. I had never owned a horse but rented a couple here and there. I had found Cor while I was riding a horse, but that had been over a year ago and I was glad I found him because I didn't know what I was doing with that horse. They were majestic beasts that I both admired and feared. I had a feeling their horses were quite tame and listened to their owners. Whether they would listen to me, however, was another story.

Would we be able to escape? Or were we going to get shot down and arrested? I supposed, either way, we would be heading to Cor if we got arrested. That, or we would be killed. Neither of those worse-case scenarios sounded fun at the moment.

And I was not looking forward to going to the estate because my father also lived there.

Would he be there currently? I had no idea. I hadn't talked to him in years. If I wasn't mistaken, the last time I saw my father wahen when I was just a toddler. I remembered a man with brown hair and light eyes, kneeling down to me, telling me everything would be all right. Then I never heard or saw him again. I, of course, saw my uncle more than I cared to. Now I understood why.

Because Byron was planting all the seeds to

destroy this world.

Byron had said that my father turned his back on what their grandfather tried to establish. If that was the case, why hadn't my father done anything about Byron? Why did he let Byron keep on trying to destroy all the nations? Why did he let Byron kill my mother—his wife?

Pain shot through my chest. I needed to stop thinking about those things—I needed to focus on the present and help my friends get out of there. We had to go and help Cor before Byron did anything horrible to him. Well, worse than he already has done, if that was even possible.

We made our way through the city I had grown fond of. Thornburg was where Cor and I spent a lot of our time, although we did move around sometimes. I knew where Byron's home was because I wanted to stay as far away from it as possible. Well, that wasn't entirely true. I wanted to talk to my father but never had the guts to do so— both because I didn't know what to say and because I didn't want to deal with Byron.

Once we got near the border of the city, Ellie

pulled the horse aside and jumped down. She had two guns with her, both I assumed were filled with tranks, and was readying them for whatever she had planned.

"Gabe, when I distract them, I need you to lead Kevin straight through the border. Don't hesitate—just run. Zach and I will be right behind. Zach, I need you to circle around so I can jump on. Think you can handle that?"

"I mean, it failed last time, but sure," Zach whispered.

I didn't like the sound of that.

Ellie let out a breath. "Which is why I'm not going to do the same thing as last time. Besides, we have someone to take Kevin. That was half the problem."

Zach shrugged, as if he didn't want to argue with Ellie but also knew this place was going to fail. "Sure, sure. Let's get this over with."

Ellie turned to the border patrol, her two guns at the ready. I gulped as I watched her begin to shoot. This could not end well. I knew I had only one job to do, but I didn't even know if her horse was going to listen to me.

She took down four of them before they started to open fire on her. She dived behind a few crates. Zach shouted behind me.

"Gabe, go!"

I couldn't believe it. They wanted me to head straight toward the border? Really? During this shoot out? This was not going to end well. I snapped the reins, and Kevin took off like it was a matter of life and death. It seemed he understood his masters better than I did. I could only imagine the things this horse had seen and experienced, and how many times he and Char had saved their masters' behinds. Kevin galloped toward the border as the patrol yelled for me to stop. I didn't. Luckily they were more preoccupied with Ellie, who was still shooting at them, to care about me galloping past. It wasn't as if I was a threat to their life at the moment.

I didn't turn back around until I couldn't hear any more shooting. Kevin seemed to understand as well as he began to slow down once he felt we were in the clear. I glanced behind me to see two people on a horse a little way away. I assumed it was Ellie and Zach, but at that distance, I couldn't be too sure. It was too far to make out Zach's bright red hair. The area was wooded, so I made a turn where there were some big bushes and rocks and waited for them to pass. Sure enough, it was Zach and Ellie.

"How did you manage all that? How did you two not get killed?" I asked as Ellie jumped off Zach's horse.

She shrugged. "A bit of luck, a bit of having to do it before. We better keep moving though—I have a feeling they're going to send a search party out for us if they haven't already."

Ellie hopped up on Kevin, and I scooted back some so she could take the reins. We kept a moderate pace through the woods and went off the path a bit. I wasn't sure what was safer, staying on the path and hoping the patrol didn't find us or going off the path and hoping bandits didn't find us.

The sun was beginning to set, and Ellie and Zach found a large rock we could keep our backs to and sleep. I wasn't sure if I had ever slept outside before like this—with no tent or blankets to put down. It was rather strange having had so many new experiences in the past week than I had almost all my life. I had also never been in jail before, and sleeping in there was definitely worse than sleeping under the stars.

As long as some rogues didn't show up and try to kill us.

"Hey, Gabe," Ellie said. "Want to help me find some wood for the fire?"

I blinked, coming back to reality and my fears vanishing away. "Yeah, I can help."

"Zach, you stay here and watch over the horses."

"All right," Zach said as he patted his horse Char.

Ellie and I made our way through the woods, searching for any broken branches and picking them up as we moved around.

"Do you think we'll be able to save him?" I asked as the silence was killing me.

Ellie shrugged. "I don't even know if we're going to make it out alive. But we might as well try. The world wouldn't be worth living if we turned our backs on what is going on. I mean, neither of us will be allowed to survive anywhere either way."

She had a point there. Unless we wanted to stay in these woods, neither of our kinds were going to be able to go into a city. "Then I guess the better question is, do you think we'll be able to stop Byron?"

She took a deep breath and let it out slowly. "I don't think we can stop him alone. We can try to kill him, but that might not be the answer. He has followers that will probably take his place. No, we'll need more people helping us, and I don't know if that will be even possible."

She had a point. I bent down and grabbed a couple more sticks. "It would have been nice if we were able to get the Sirians to side with us, but that didn't end well. All that is left are the Lyrans, but I don't think we have any way to talk to anyone high up. Besides, weren't you wanted in the Lyran Zone?"

"I think by this point we're wanted everywhere. After we get Cor, we'll have to travel north and lie low to figure it all out for a while."

"In the mountains, you mean?"

Ellie nodded. "Yeah. We'll need supplies though. I'm not sure how we're going to go about it. Maybe we could get a bunch of supplies before breaking Byron's estate. Pack everything up on the horses and have them ready to go. Maybe some med kits as well, in case Cor is in worse shape than when we left him."

I felt bad for Cor. He had been shot, but we had to run. If we stayed, then we would all be at Byron's mercy. There would be no way we would have all escaped once we were in his grasp. The problem was, would we be any better off after we broke in to save Cor?

"My father is in the estate with Byron. It's possible he's living there now. Byron said that he had turned his back on the plan by marry my mother, but I don't know. He left when I was little. I don't know if we can trust him."

"But he might be our way in is what you're saying?" Ellie asked.

I slowly nodded. "Or he could turn on us, and

we'll be going straight into a trap."

"It's still an idea. Do you think you could get a message to him without Byron knowing?"

That was a good question. "I'm not sure. We could wait outside the building until he comes out in a carriage to visit the town, but I'm not sure how often he leaves the estate or if he's even there."

"It's worth a shot. Come on, let's get back to camp. This is enough wood, and we can tell Zach our idea."

CHAPTER VIII

Ellie

This was going to work. It had to. Or else, we were all screwed.

I knew it wouldn't. I knew something would go wrong. It always did. We were all lucky that none of us hadn't died yet. We found ourselves in the worst situations, yet we always seemed to make it out alive. One of these days, however, it wasn't going to end up like that. One of these days, we were going to die and that would be that.

For some reason that didn't bother me. I didn't want to die—far from it—but after everything, it just felt like an acceptance. We had faced so much death and destruction—it almost felt like second nature now. Or perhaps I was just numb because that was how my mind delt with it all. But if this was the way we were going to go, then so be it. At least we were trying to make a difference. At least we stood up for what was right.

Even though I had friends, I felt alone on this planet, and I had a feeling they did as well. It almost seemed like it was us against the world. Part of me wanted to give up—part of me wanted to run off to the mountains and never look back. If we did that, however, they would eventually come looking for us. By the sounds of it, Byron would do anything to take us out. But would he travel all the way into the mountains? Would he even be able to find us?

Sure he would. He had the money and therefore the manpower to do it. Just like he had the manpower to destroy all the other races.

It was disgusting.

I knew that not all humans wanted that. In fact, I doubted even ninety-nine percent wanted that. But none of them did anything about it. They either didn't know what was going on or they were blind to it. Either way, that made it so Byron could do whatever he wanted. Then he convinced his followers he was right and that the other nations were out to destroy the humans.

And it really did appear like that.

If I were a human and didn't know better, I would have believed it too. On the outside, it looked like the Silurians had killed all those people up on the moon base of Zynon. The Silurians didn't like any other nation, so it wouldn't have been surprising they attacked. However, that wasn't what happened. Byron had forced Zach to transform into the leader of the Silurians and ordered them to attack everyone else at the casino, leading to many deaths. Luckily Zach was able to escape with us, but that meant Byron had been after us since that moment, and he was going to stop at nothing to capture us.

Which brought us up to the present.

"So what do you think?" I asked Zach as we sat around the fire. Although most of the time a fire brought attention to one's location, with the large hillside and how deep we were in the woods, it was doubtful anyone would spot us. It was cold, and we needed the warmth. For tonight, we could risk it.

Zach shook his head. "I don't think there will be any way we can do this without endangering our lives."

"But we have to stop him. We have to figure out a way to take down Byron and to save Cor."

"So you want to assassinate Byron?" Zach eyed me.

I shrugged. "Might as well try. He wants us dead. Let's just return the favor."

"And what if that is part of his plan?" Zach asked. "What if he's willing to be a martyr, knowing that our plan may kill him? He could have it all set up, showing that other races and half humans want all humans dead or something."

He had a point there. He probably had a million backup plans. I rubbed my forehead as I tried to think of a way out of this.

"The only way to stop all this is to get the humans, or maybe the Lyrans, to understand what is going on. If we can get one of them to understand the truth behind Byron, then perhaps we can stop him," Gabe commented as he stirred the stew we had going. Zach was able to catch some rabbits, and I was able to find some leaves that would make a good stock.

I took a deep breath. "I wouldn't expect anyone to believe us. None of us are the sort of people that anyone believes. The entire planet turned on my people, and you are a runaway prince. If they find out who you are, they might turn you in to the Sirians."

Gabe was quiet. He knew I had a point.

"I still don't think we'll even be able to get close to the estate without getting arrested," Zach went on. "Cor has a better chance of escaping on his own than us saving his ass again. Let's be honest, over the past few days, he has been the damsel in distress, and we have had to step in to help him."

I shook my head. "Don't forget I have had to

come help you out of bad situations, and Gabe is always stuck in some kind of pickle. I'm actually the only damsel, and I'm that is saving everyone else's ass.

Zach chuckled. "Fair point. It's almost as if no one wants to deal with you."

I shot him a look. "Watch your tongue. It's not because they don't want to deal with me—it's because they know better than to mess with me."

"It's that resting bitch face," Zach whispered with a grin.

"You know that's right."

Gabe simply listened to us as he stared into the fire. He stirred the stew almost unconsciously, lost in his own thoughts. I knew that look—it was the look of complete mental shut down.

"You all right, Gabe?" I asked.

He blinked and glanced up at me. He shrugged. "Can anyone be all right? There are so many problems in the world. It feels as if they'll never be fixed. At least, not in our lifetime, if ever. Sometimes I wonder what the point is and if this world is even worth fighting for."

Zach and I were silent as we both had the same feeling. We had lost almost everything. The world wasn't fair, and neither of us would be surprised if all the races on this world would doom themselves. All but the Pleiadians, of course. They had isolated themselves on some island and didn't let anyone in except those who traded wine with them. They knew not to mess with any other race. Perhaps after we all destroyed ourselves, they would take what was left and build a new empire or something of the sort.

But that would be after our time, so it didn't matter. Gabe had a point. Why did we care? Couldn't we just run off and hide? I didn't want to do that without Cor, however, and if we were going to get Cor, then we were going to find ourselves right in the middle of whatever Byron was planning next. Not to mention even if we tried to go hide, it was more than likely that Byron would search the ends of the world for us just to make us suffer. He had a personal vendetta for each and every one of us, whether we liked it or not.

"I don't have an answer for that, Gabe, but we

need to save Cor either way," I said. "So how exactly do you think we'll be able to get inside without Byron knowing or capturing us right away?"

Gabe stopped stirring the stew. "Well, presuming my father is there, I could send a letter to him from the town. Although Byron likes to control everything, I doubt he reads my father's messages. Once that happens, well, we wait for a response."

"So we're going to risk our necks, hoping your father isn't an asshole like Byron. No offense," Zach commented.

Gabe sighed. "None taken. I don't know. When I talked to Byron… he said my father was a traitor and went against all their grandfather's beliefs. If that was the case, if my father loved my mother, then we can trust him, right? I mean, he had me, and I'm what Byron despises most. So I presume that he doesn't agree with Byron and that he would help us."

Zach and I glanced at each other. That made a little sense, but there was still a big hole in that logic.

"Then why does he live with Byron?" Zach asked before I could. "If they don't agree with each other, then why would he be there?"

Gabe shrugged. "I really don't know. He left when I was little, but my mother would always talk about how sweet he was. I mean, if he was there to keep Byron in check or perhaps because my father is the eldest and he takes care of the estate."

I shook my head. "He's not keeping Byron in check though. For all we know, he could be on Byron's side and helping him."

"Then I'll go to him alone and the two of you find a different way in. I'll help us, then I'll get ahold of you. If he betrays me, well, then at least I'll be arrested with Cor and I'll finally know where my father stands with all this."

Zach and I looked at each other. It was the best plan we could come up with. Zach and I would just have to find another way in. Simple as that.

Or at least as simple as most of our life was.

CHAPTER IX

Cor

Well, this sucked.

I would have preferred being in a celled wagon than simply cuffed at the ankles and wrists with a chain tying me to the bottom of the carriage. While the celled wagon made it so people could throw stuff at me, which wasn't that big of a deal since I already knew everyone hated me, having to sit across from Byron as he gave me a satisfied smirk was torture.

All I wanted in this life was this man dead.

No, death was too kind. I wanted to see this man suffer. I wanted to watch him as everything he worked so hard for fell apart. I wanted him to watch as the loved ones around him suffered just like I like I had to. He deserved the worst punishments that could be given to a man. Death was too easy for that son of a bitch.

We rode through the city and toward the border patrol. I had no idea if Ellie, Zach, and Gabe were still in the city or if they decided to escape. Did they know where Byron was going to take me? Or did they just run for their lives, leaving me behind to figure a way out by myself? Was I ever going to see them again?

Was I going to die?

Byron didn't want me dead. No, he wanted to rub salt in an open wound. He wanted me to see the destruction I had a hand in. He wanted me to see what the simple act of giving the codes to the Kausian shields had escalated to. He was evil incarnated, and I could do nothing to stop him.

No—that wasn't true. I would just have to sacrifice myself in the process.

I knew that was what it would take to stop him. There would be some moment where I could kill him, but it would cost me my life. At least, that was how I always imagined it. Although I wanted him to suffer, I knew that wasn't going to be easy, if even possible. No, I would have to make it quick, I was sure he would take me down with him.

I never imagined what my life would be like after getting my revenge. I had always assumed I would die either when I killed Krax or Ellie would find me and kill me. She tried almost a week ago to do just that, and I was prepared to face her wrath. But instead, she listened to my story and, for some reason, forgave me.

I didn't deserve her forgiveness, and we both knew that. Zach was less convinced that I was innocent, and I didn't blame him. I was far from innocent between what happened to Kaus and all the things I had . I should have let them kill me—I should have never caved and given them those codes. But I never could have imagined this was what was going to happen.

We all knew that people hated the Kausians because they could transform into any other race, but to kill us all… It was unimaginable. I thought they would just take over the zone and make us part of their citizenship. Things were already horrible for us. I couldn't imagine it much worse.

But I was clearly wrong.

"What's with that scowl? Are you really that surprised I caught up to you yet again?" Byron asked.

I glared at him but didn't say anything. There was honestly nothing I had to say to him. He knew my anger—he just wanted to get even further under my skin. And he was succeeding.

"Well, if you aren't going to talk, I'll simply talk for you. If you are wondering if your friends are going to make it out alive, don't you fret. I'll have them in my grasp in no time."

He paused, as if thinking that would get me to talk. I simply kept staring at him.

"They'll come for you because they value other people's lives over their own. And I'll be ready this time. There is no way they'll escape."

I felt my lip curl a little. Byron noticed it.

"Oh? You don't think they'll come for you? Do you think they finally left you for good?"

I didn't say anything, but that was exactly how I felt. They shouldn't come back for me. They would be idiots. They had their freedom—they needed to hold on to it. They could hide in the woods or even the mountains up north. They have their freedom. Why would they risk that just to help me?

I wasn't worth their potential harm.

I was the one who'd brought all this on. I was the one who'd thought I could get my revenge. If I had just stayed with Ellie and Zach after the attack—if I had never believed that some human wanted me to live a better life—we would have been fine. But no, I was selfish and wanted more out of this world. I should have stuck with what the cards were handed to me when I was born.

It was more than likely Byron would still have gotten what he wanted and declared war on the Kausians, then later war on the Silurians. He was more than likely going to attack the Lyrans next.

He had the Sirians under control as I doubted any of them were going to leave the sea now. It would be a matter of time before the Sirians who lived in the other zones would either return to the ocean or be considered outliers and eradicated from the Human Zone. I assumed Byron didn't care about the humans in the other zones and would let them die during the attacks. He probably branded them as traitors to their kind anyway.

Byron was twisted, and while I wanted to believe he was the only human who viewed the world the way he did, I knew I was largely mistaken. There were plenty of humans and other races that viewed the world the same way Byron did. Most of them had the money and power to put those plans into action. It was sickening, to say the least.

"Well, I know they'll come for you," Byron commented. "That boy Gabriel has too soft of a heart even though he grew up utterly alone. Perhaps he's just attached to you because you are the first person who ever cared about him."

"Don't you ever say his name. You don't deserve to talk about him," I growled. "You are the reason his entire zone hates him. You are the reason he ran away from home and now is wanted for murdering his own mother."

Byron shifted in his seat. "Oh, so that comment made you talk? I'm surprised—I didn't think you actually cared about him. I figured he was just something to keep you busy. Isn't it Elvira that you care for? I mean, she's the reason you took my help. You wanted to make a difference for her, and it is safe to say you did."

I looked out to the window. He was wrong. Gabe wasn't just a distraction from Ellie. I cared about him, but I also still cared about her. I didn't know what to do.

Byron leaned forward. "What, do you not care for her anymore? Are you just using her to keep Gabe safe? She's a strong one, I'll give you that. Had I known she was going to be such a pain in my ass, I wouldn't have hired her to assassinate Gabe."

I turned back to face him. "So you knew who she was when you hired her?"

"Of course. I thought maybe in her wrath she would kill you too. Then you both would be out of my hair."

"Then why are we still alive? You had plenty of chances to kill us. Why keep us alive?"

Byron smiled. "Perhaps I have grown soft. I did care for you for a couple of years, you know. And Gabriel is my nephew after all."

"So you want us to live to watch your world be created, only to kill us after it all went down. Because you are selfless like that?"

"Precisely. I do all of this out of kindness. You should thank me."

I shook my head. "You are unbelievable. You know none of this will work, right? You are going to die, and hopefully it is by my hand."

He held up his arms as if shrugging. "It doesn't matter to me if I live or not. I just want my plan to succeed. Once the pieces are in place, it really doesn't matter."

"So you believe yourself to be a martyr."

"If push comes to shove. But I don't think it will be necessary. I have a lot of people watching my back. And now that you know killing me won't stop anything, I doubt you and your friends will try.

Not without having to take down an entire army of people."

I turned back to look outside as we made it to the border. Stopping him was going to take a lot more work than I thought.

CHAPTER X

Zach

Why were we even bothering?

I didn't want to say that out loud or else I would have seemed like a dick. I cared about Cor, or at least I did when we were younger. But now with everything that had happened and everything that was going on, I didn't know what to think.

Was it possible to care and not care for someone at the same time?

It had been only three years since we saw him last, and now we were risking our lives for him. That didn't seem fair, at least not to me. He wasn't the same person he was back then—none of us were. We all had changed because of the attack and all the events that had happened after that. So then why was it that Ellie cared for him so much?

I knew the answer to that. It was because she wanted to believe he was the same person he was when we knew him. She wanted everything to go back to how it was, but that wasn't possible. Our home was gone and most of the people with it. There was no way that many Kausians survived. She needed to stop lying to herself.

If there was a big group of Kausians, we would know about it. All the Kausians we had ever heard about were by themselves or in small family groups hiding in small towns—keeping their heads down and staying out of trouble. None of them could rebuild a community—they would be attacked immediately. The only Kausians who did cause trouble were Ellie, me, and Cor. We would have heard about them otherwise.

So she was lying to herself, thinking after all this was done, she would live happily ever after. I knew deep down she understood the truth of the situation, but her heart wanted to think otherwise. And I couldn't blame her—I wanted more than anything to go back to a time where we were all happy together even if deep down we knew life was one big hardship.

Then there was the whole thing with Gabe. Did Cor really think he could just keep leading them both on? Or did he plan to marry them both after all this was over? I didn't understand what he was thinking. Did he actually care about them, or did he just not know how to handle telling someone no?

I let out a sigh as I climbed up on my horse Char. The sun had already begun to rise in the distance, and we had finished packing everything up. I watched as Gabe climbed up on the horse behind Ellie. They were both small, and Kevin was a bit bigger than Char. They fit fine. It hurt to ride without a saddle though, so Ellie was able to use some of our blankets for Gabe to sit on. It would help some, but he was still going to be sore by the time we made it to town.

"Ready?" Ellie asked as she brought her horse Kevin over to me.

I nodded. "As ready as I'll ever be."

"We'll get through this, Zach. Don't you worry."

I nodded. Sure we would. It wasn't as if a madman was out there who wanted to torture us or anything. It wasn't as if he were crazy and had forced Cor to kill all his people and forced me to start the attack on the Silurians. Nope—nothing to worry about.

Ellie led the way since I, well, really sucked at directions. She made it seem so easy, but there was no way I knew where I was going. All the mountains and hills looked the same to me, and even if I were to use a compass, I would end up going in the completely wrong direction. I had no idea what would happen if Ellie wasn't with me. I would probably end up on the moon when I was just trying to go to the building next door.

When the path widened, I brought my horse next to Ellie's. Gabe turned to me and smiled.

"You look lonely. Do you want me to ride with

you next time?"

I blushed. Since we first met, he kept hitting on me. Since I knew he didn't mean anything by it, I didn't mind. It was just how he was. Besides, he was saying that more than likely because he noticed I was thinking about everything that was going to happen.

"Ellie is a lot better on her horse than I am. You are safer there. I have Char to keep me company."

"She's a pretty horse," Gabe commented.

"Kevin is more handsome," Ellie interjected. "And he's stronger."

"What Char lacks in strength she makes up in agility."

Ellie nodded. "That is true. But they are both very fast. They have gotten us out of a lot of messes."

"I can imagine," Gabe said. "You two seem to always be in some sort of mess or another."

I let out a sigh. "You can say that again. And it doesn't seem the pattern is going to change ever."

"It's our lot in life, Zach. It always has been," Ellie commented.

I knew she was right. Even when we lived in Kaus, we were always in trouble and had people after us. Between the stunts we would pull and the fact that no other race liked us, we always had to watch our backs. That never changed.

But when we were headed into trouble like this, I always got nervous. Most of our marks had always been someone that wasn't so high up in society. What sort of backlash would we get if we did end up killing him? Would they all side with him, or would they believe us when we said it was self-defense?

As if anyone would believe us.

We had learned over the years that no matter how innocent we were in an accident or fight, we were the ones who got blamed. This usually led to us running as fast as we could. My leg muscles were quite strong after everything we had been through, and so were Ellie's. We could even outrun a Lyran, which was known to be the fastest race. Silurians were the slowest, but they were clever in how they cornered people. They also carried the most weapons.

They wouldn't be in our hair—at least not for a while. I wondered how their zone was doing after everything that had happened. It had only been a few days, so it couldn't be too bad. Then again, Kaus had been destroyed in a matter of minutes. I don't think Byron would have been able to completely wipe them out, but he might have started a war of sorts.

I didn't feel that bad for the Silurians—especially since they were the ones who led the attack on Kaus. They weren't very innocent and hated all the other races. They only played nice because they could get something out of deals and trades. It still shouldn't be like this, however.

If we were successful or someone else was successful in stopping Byron, the entire world was going to be a mess to clean up, if cleaning it all up was even possible. The Sirians had turned their back on the rest of the world; no one trusted the Silurians even before everything went down, and the Kausians were near extinct. Perhaps simply getting our revenge was our best option and we could just move forward from that.

We ventured farther through the woods toward the next town that Gabe had said Byron would be in. I tried not to think about what was awaiting us and how I doubted Cor would have come to save us if he were the only one who escaped. I thought about how after we saved Cor, if we succeeded of course, we could finally be free of all this nonsense. I had a feeling, however, that wasn't how it was going to go down.

As we kept moving, the suns got higher in the sky, and I was glad the trees provided some shade as it was getting rather hot. We were able to fill our canteens with water from a stream and filtered it through a doohickey we had been carrying for forever. Luckily a lot of our travel stuff was stored with the horses, so we didn't have to worry about getting new ones.

After a couple more hours, I could see the town itself. I took in a deep breath and let it out slowly. This was it. There was no turning back now.

CHAPTER XI

Gabe

This was going to work. I had to keep telling myself that.

My father would help us—he had to. There was no way he could be helping Byron. He loved my mother and my mother loved him with all her heart. She always spoke of his kindness and the little things he did for her when they first me. If he was aligned with Byron, then why would he be in a relationship with someone who wasn't a human?

Byron had claimed that my father had betrayed their grandfather, so he would hear us out and help us. I was sure of it. I wasn't sure why he never bothered to visit me when I was living with my mother or why he was living with Byron, but there had to be an explanation. He had to be better than him and would help us talk to the Lyran Zone. We would save Cor, and then we would save this planet.

I took a few deep breaths as we came to the edge of the town. The capital was guarded with the borders, but many of the smaller towns did not have that. Byron had homes in a few cities, but his big estate was in this town. I had never visited the mansion, but my mother would talk about it when I was younger. I had once come to the town, however, but chickened out about seeing my dad. It was half because I didn't know what I would say to him and the other half because I didn't want Byron to know where I was. I had been right all along about him wanting to kill me, although that wasn't a big surprise.

While the town wasn't surrounded by walls, the large estates that the richer people in the zone had were. They all had their own personal security, but at least we would be able to stop in the town and grab something good to eat. The rabbit stew last night didn't really hit the spot, mainly because I couldn't stop thinking about their cute, fuzzy faces before Zach prepped them for the meal. I didn't watch as I knew I would not have the stomach.

Ellie led us into the town. I noticed she glanced around, probably checking to make sure there weren't any Wanted posters up or people on the lookout for us. So far, no one seemed to pay us much mind, which was even more worrisome.

"So far so good," she whispered. "But keep your eyes out for anything suspicious. I don't believe for a moment that he doesn't have people searching for us, not to mention Wanted posters more than likely fill this area."

"Remind me again why we didn't just stay in the woods."

"Because hiding in plain sight is sometimes easier than dealing with bandits."

She had a point there. A few months ago, Cor and I had to deal with bandits that attacked our train. It was not fun. Luckily Cor dealt with them and they were arrested when the law enforcement arrived. It was still something I didn't want to relive.

Ellie took her horse to the stables. She jumped off the horse, and I followed suit. I didn't land as smoothly as she did, however.

"Ow…," I said as I bent down, my legs and hips hurting more than I could ever imagine.

Zach hopped off his horse and patted my back. "There, there. It will get better… eventually."

I had never ridden bareback on a horse before, and now I knew why. With as much effort as I could muster, I moved one leg forward and then the other.

Ellie and Zach talked to the man in charge of the stables, Ellie's left hand never moving far from her gun. I searched around, trying to find anything out of the ordinary, but I saw nothing. What was Byron plotting?

He was more than likely back now since we took the long way around to this town. Byron had guards and carriages with multiple horses. He would have no trouble using the main road. So he had time to prepare.

"What do you have in store for us, you bastard?" I whispered as I rubbed my thighs. They weren't getting much better. I wanted to sit down, but I knew the odds of me being able to get up after sitting wasn't going to be an option. I tried stretching them out and stepping around a little bit.

Nope. I was just going to have to deal with this for a while.

I let out a sigh as Ellie and Zach finished and met up with me.

"Sorry, Gabe," Ellie commented. "After this is all said and done, we'll either get you your own horse or perhaps a two-person saddle."

"Another horse would be better," Zach said. "Less weight for one horse and they can run faster."

"That is true." Ellie sighed. "But I don't think we can afford one."

"I might be able to afford one if my account hasn't been locked down yet," I interjected.

"We can check, but wherever we check, we'll have to make a run for it," Ellie said as she patted my shoulder. "Not that we don't usually have to already."

She could say that again.

"Let's go find a place to stay. I think Byron is letting us come to him this time. I haven't noticed anything out of the ordinary," I said as I turned to the street. I moved my leg a little too much and grimaced. I hoped I wouldn't have to do any sort of running anytime soon.

The motel for the town wasn't that far from the stables, not that the town was that large anyway. There was quite the economic difference between the people who lived and worked in the town versus the houses that were scattered on the outside of it. I noticed some of the folk who had houses came in to either shop or whatnot, but it was clear this was their countryside residence and they conducted all their business in the larger cities. Seeing such differences in how people lived always fascinated and disgusted me. I grew up within the palace walls and never realized how hard people had it on the outside. Although I knew I would never rule, if I had, I would try to fix it all. I doubted I would have been successful, however, as there were many factors that played into economics —all of which were ridiculous.

"Let's stop here," Zach said, bringing me out of my thoughts. I turned to him and examined the place we would be staying. Yes, I was used to the finer things in life, and as I peered at the building, I immediately prayed to the goddess that I wouldn't get bitten by some ticks or nibbled on by rats.

I didn't say any of that as I followed the others inside to the lobby. Cor and I usually stayed in some nice places, mainly because that was where people who paid the most stayed, which in turn would earn us more money. I kept close to Zach, hoping he would save me from the vermin that scuttled across the floor.

Zach and Ellie didn't seem to be bothered by any of it. I understood why they were so interested in the bed when we were on the ship to Zynon what seemed to be years ago but had only been a little over a week. I would crave a bed as well after living like we had for the past couple of days. A bed that was soft and didn't have bugs in it.

I really hoped it wouldn't take that long to save Cor.

As Ellie dealt with the man behind the counter, I glanced around. I didn't notice any Wanted signs of us. Byron hadn't set us up nor had news traveled from the capital, pinning that bombing on us. I had noticed over the past couple of years that news didn't travel between towns like one would assume. I had always found it odd but now found it to be quite handy.

That explained why Ellie and Zach were able to work as bounty hunters without risking getting shot every time they stepped into a town.

Well, it seemed that was still an issue, but that was because they crossed one person or another each time they stepped into a different town. Wanted posters expired after a while, mainly because they had to be paid by someone to keep up. That didn't make much sense to me in the long run, but it seemed to work to our advantage, so I didn't think about it too much.

Ellie turned with a key in hand. "Looks like we got a bottom floor."

"Is that good?" I asked.

"It's easier to escape from," Zach commented. "Hypothetically, at least. You don't have to deal with stairs or jumping off buildings."

"Speak from experience?"

Both of them nodded in unison. "Yup."

I held back my laugh as we headed outside and around the building. There were little patios for each room, but that was about it. Ellie stopped in front of a room that had a window with a broken screen and unlocked the door.

Two rats ran out of the room, and I screamed like a little girl.

CHAPTER XII

Ellie

Gabe screamed at a higher pitch than Zach did.

Boys were such crybabies. I scanned the room for a broom and forced the rest of the rats to leave the room. They had all these muscles, had dealt with people trying to kill them, but always screamed when there was a rat. I knew rats weren't harmless, but out of all the things we dealt with, they weren't the worst things to come across.

After gathering himself, Zach went and checked the bathroom. In our experience, there was someone hiding in our bathroom thirty percent of the time. Usually it was after we had checked in and gone out to take care of our business, but we still looked. Once in a while, the motel owner was setting us up as well.

"All clear. Well, except for some spiders and a cockroach. Not sure which one is going to win in their fight though."

I glanced in the bathroom. Sure enough, there was a cockroach and spider fighting. "I'm going to take bets on the spider. He looks gnarly."

Zach stomped on both of them. "Oh, looks like it's a draw. Zach for the win." He raised his fists in victory.

I sighed as I turned back to Gabe. Poor boy's eyes were wider than I had ever seen them before. He was not used to staying in such filth, and if we had our way, we wouldn't want to be here either. But we had to keep a low profile, and places like this made that all the more possible.

"Chin up, we won't be here long," I said as I

lifted up the sheets. "Hey, at least the bed is clean of anything."

"Are you sure? Because the rest of this place doesn't seem that great…," Gabe said as he carefully stepped to the other bed. He lifted up the sheet, and a few moths came flying out, causing him to jump back. He grimaced as he rubbed his legs.

"Don't worry. Moths are harmless."

"I know that—they just surprised me."

"You should probably sit down and let your legs rest. We have a lot of work, and you need them to be as strong as possible in case we have to make a run for it."

Gabe collapsed on the bed. I moved over to him and knelt down. "Want me to help massage them? I have a technique that Cor taught me a long while back when we used to ride and I rode behind him."

"This is going to end up as a happy-ending massage now is it? Since Cor taught you?" Gabe joked.

I laughed. "No, but his definitely do. Or at least, back in the day."

"Yeah, I believe that," Gabe commented.

I helped him massage his legs as Zach took a shower. We didn't have any pain relievers on us, and I hadn't picked up any plants on our way in. I should have been on the lookout for some, knowing Gabe would be sore like this. He wasn't used to riding horses like we were.

After a bit, Gabe nodded. "I think I feel better. Thanks."

I patted his leg as I stood up. "My pleasure. Want to test it out?"

He slowly stood up, wincing a little but not as bad as earlier. "Yeah, this is much better. Thank you."

"Do some leg stretches as well. Those will help a lot."

He began to stretch out as I collapsed on Zach and my bed. I covered my eyes with my arm and tried to think about what we were going to do next. We had to save Cor, and we had to find somewhere to hide. But where could the likes of us even hide?

"Hey, Ellie?" Gabe whispered.

I turned to look at him. "Yeah?"

"I'm scared to face my dad. Is that bad? I mean, with my mother it was different. With her, I was just afraid she wouldn't believe me and would act like I was overthinking everything. But with my dad… I haven't seen him since I was really little. I don't even remember him—all I have in my mind are pictures of him my mother kept and ones we would get with letters sometimes."

I tried to think about what my own family looked like but pushed those thoughts back. With each and every passing day, it seemed I was forgetting their faces more and more, and I didn't want to face that reality.

"I don't know what to say to that, Gabe. I hope he will help us—I hope that he's a nicer guy than Byron, but that isn't a high bar. I think odds are if he had you and loved your mom, that there is some sort of morality in him and that we might be able to convince him. It's a shot in the dark, but it could be all we have to stop Byron and to save Cor."

He smiled. "Yeah, if all else fails, I'll be a good distraction while you and Zach sneak in."

"Hopefully… but we shall see how well Zach

and I are able to sneak in. I mean, you have seen how well our missions go so far."

"But you always survive. So there's that."

"That is true. Lady Luck has been on our side. But it takes one slipup for everything to come crashing down."

"That's true for everyone though. Byron just needs to mess up for us to get the advantage."

He had a point there. I smiled. "Anyone ever tell you that you are way too optimistic for all the shit you have had to deal with in your life?"

"Cor usually says that actually. He thinks I'm easygoing for how much I deal with—and that was before he knew I was half Sirian and the son of the queen of the Sirian Zone."

He got quiet for a moment, and I let him take his time while he thought about his mom. He knew I was there for him, but sometimes one just needed a moment for it to sink in again. I had been there when we'd lost everything.

Zach stepped out of the shower, using the rag that they called a towel to dry his hair. "Who's next?"

I nodded to Gabe. "How about you go? I'll

probably take a lot less time than you to get ready, especially since you are going in to impress your father."

"Right." He stood up and went to the bathroom and closed the door.

"Should we find him some nice clothes?" Zach asked.

I shrugged. "Probably. But that would mean one of us needs to go out there."

Zach pointed at his hair. "I still need to dry this mop. I don't want to go out and catch a cold."

"Zach, it's summer and really hot out. I don't think you need to worry…"

He pouted. He really just didn't want to go shopping. I sighed as I stood up. "Good thing we have some money left over. He really does need some nicer clothes if he's going to talk to his dad. I think we're all starting to smell funky."

"We'll have to wash our clothes after you take a shower. I presume we would just clean them in the tub?"

"That sounds good. I'll be back," I said as I left the motel.

I glanced around as I stepped outside. There still didn't seem to be anyone looking for us. It made me more nervous than if there were people watching us. Byron had something up his sleeve, and I didn't know what it was. Did he think we would come right to him so he didn't waste any effort? Or was there something else going on? Knowing him, it was probably the former.

The tailor wasn't that far from the motel, mainly because the town was small and everything was nearby. I stepped inside to find a few suits and dresses available. I wrinkled my nose at the dresses. I did not want to be wearing another one of those anytime soon.

"Can I help you?" an elderly man asked. His graying hair contrasted with his dark skin, and he smiled brightly. He appeared to like his job.

"I need a suit for my friend. Nothing too fancy— just something clean and presentable."

He examined me up and down. "Well, if he's in any shape you are in, I can understand why he needs new clothes. What are his dimensions?"

Crap, I didn't ask. "He's slender and probably

not too much bigger than me."

"I have a few suits in small sizes that he will probably fit then. If not, you can come back and exchange them later today." He flipped through the suits that were hanging up. "How about this one?"

The suit was green and reminded me of the hat he had when we met him. "I think that will do. Thank you." I handed him the cash.

"My pleasure. I hope you come in again."

I gave him a nod as I carried the suit back to the hotel. As I made my way to the others, I noticed a man walking around, peering in all the shops. He appeared similar to Byron but a bit different. His body shape was different—almost like… Gabe's.

That was him—that was Gabe's father.

CHAPTER XIII

Cor

At least this was better than the prison cell. Much better, to be honest.

I glanced out the barred window down at the dozen or so guards that were circling the premises. There was no way I was going to escape by breaking through the window and crawling down the side of the mansion. I had better odds going through the front door.

Which brought me back to examining the door. It was made of metal, which wasn't too hard to break if I had a way to pick a lock, but I didn't. Not because I didn't have a pick, but because there was no way to access the lock from this side. It was completely flush on this side of the room. I had no idea how old this estate was, but whoever had built this had one thing in mind—they didn't want anyone to escape.

I sighed as I examined the rest of the room. I had my bed, which was nice. I also had a bathroom that had a curtain so at least I had some privacy if someone walked in. There were a couple of vents for cool air and heat, but it was tiny and there was no way I could even fit my head in it.

Stepping back to the window, I opened it up with the lever. It was nice to have some fresh air, but there were still the metal bars. I could theoretically bend them if I tried hard enough, but I doubted I would have been able to fit, not to mention there were still all the guards down below. And they all had guns on them.

I sat down on the bed. It was comfortable, which

was a lot more than I had ever been provided. In fact, it was one of the most comfortable beds I had ever slept on. Last night, I slept like a log. I felt bad as I knew that the others were probably camping out in the middle of nowhere, having to keep watch for any bandits or if the law enforcement from the city were out looking for them. But that clearly didn't keep me up last night.

There was a small hatch at the bottom of the door that the guards could open and slide food in, which they had done for me at breakfast and lunch. Byron hadn't stepped in here to try to get on my nerves today, which I was thankful for. I really didn't want to deal with him anytime soon.

But the question still stood—how was I going to get out of this? Were the others coming for me? I doubted it since they would be stupid to risk their lives for me. I didn't deserve that. No, I deserved to rot in a prison a lot worse than this one.

Ellie and Zach made it clear that they weren't going to come for me. Would Gabe try to on his own, or would he hide with the other two? He should stay hidden—Byron had made it appear as if he had killed his own mom—the queen of the Sirian Zone. If anyone found him, he would be executed. I wasn't worth his life. I wasn't worth any of their lives.

And yet, I held on to hope that someone would save me.

I knew I was alone, though. I had always been alone. I was an only child, and my parents were hardly at home. The only person who cared about me growing up was Ellie and ach, but I had betrayed them. I deserved to be alone. Everyone after that I met was just using me for sex. None of it meant a thing because I no longer could feel anything.

That is, until I met Gabe.

Sure, I was using him in the beginning, but he grew on me quickly. He was naïve in many ways, but that's what made me love him. In the beginning, he was using me as well, so while I felt a little bad about my initial intentions, I knew it was mutual.

But even with him I didn't have a long-term plan.

So, he should leave me behind. He deserved better. They all did. I started this mess and I needed to be the one who would get myself out. It was as simple as that.

Standing back up, I began to move around. The one thing a lot of people didn't realize about solitary confinement like this was the importance to have to keep moving so you didn't lose your muscles. It had only been a day, but I didn't like keeping still. I moved to the floor and started doing crunches. I couldn't let myself get weak even if it had only been a couple of days between this cell and the last. I needed to be at my best in order to take down Byron.

What I really wanted more than anything was a shower. It had been a while. I at least had taken some of my layers off, but I was beginning to smell. There was no bath in the restroom, and there was only a sink that sputtered a little water with a push sensor for the faucet. I had already tried to break it apart so I could flood the room, but it was foolproof. They had thought of everything.

It could be worse, I kept telling myself. It could be a lot worse.

Other than the fact I had been captured and had

to witness a madman try to destroy the world. That part of it all wasn't that great. But he could have thrown me in a basement with rats and bugs while it all happened. So there was that.

I wondered if Gabe and the others would have been given separate rooms or if they would have thrown us all in here. I assumed they would have separated us so we couldn't plan anything. That was what I would have done, at least.

The door made an unlatching sound, and I quickly stood up, almost pulling an ab muscle. That was always the worst muscle to pull, I swore.

As the door opened, I saw two guards and then Byron with a smile on his face. I gave him a glare, but it only made him laugh.

"Why are you so upset? Don't you like your accommodations? And weren't the meals excellent?"

I had to admit it, the food had been good. But that didn't make up for everything else he was doing. "Just kill me and get it over with. I don't want to be your plaything to amuse you."

He laughed again. "So quick to want to die.

Believe me, Cornelius, you are much more than a plaything to me. Contrary to what you believe, I really did care about you when I was helping you study. You had a lot of potential—a lot more than other Kausians I had worked with."

I frowned. "So I wasn't the first?"

"Does that make you jealous? No, you weren't the first I worked with to try to get into your city, but you certainly were the last. I did have to act like I was partnered with that Silurian Krax, however. I'd much rather work with a Kausian than the likes of them."

"And yet you partnered with them for how long?" I asked.

He shrugged. "It was part of the plan. I couldn't really go against my plan, now could I?"

I shook my head. "No, I suppose you can't. But it wasn't part of your precious plan for me to still be alive. Nor Gabe. So you don't always go by the book, do you?"

Byron smirked. "I'm going to miss you, you know that? I love our banter. It's so clever. It must be all training you got."

I glared at him. I wanted to reiterate that I was good at back-talking way before he came along, but I decided not to. I wouldn't give him that pleasure.

"Now come. I want you to have afternoon tea with me."

I stared at him blankly. "You trust me not to escape?"

"I think you would be wise to not try to escape. Besides, don't you want to find out if your friends are going to save you or not?"

With that, he turned and headed down the corridor. I frowned as I followed him. He had a point—I did want to know if they were going to try to help me. I knew the odds were slim and that they would be risking their lives to try to help me. No one was that stupid, were they? Then again, Ellie could be stubborn. But she was the one who said they had a pact to not go back for someone—not when it was too dangerous. It was more important to stay alive so they could stop Byron. They wouldn't come for me. No, I needed to find a way out of here on my own.

As we went down the hallway, I glanced around,

careful to note where the guards were, windows, doors, and what rooms. Up on this floor it seemed there were a lot of guards and the doors were mostly closed. Were there other people being held captive? Or was it all to intimidate me? It seemed a lot of work to mess with my mind, but I wouldn't put it past Byron to do such a thing.

I heard someone scream from down the hallway. Perhaps I was wrong—perhaps there were people behind those doors. I gulped as I heard Byron chuckle.

"Don't worry. I won't hurt you. Not unless you force me to."

What kind of sadistic place was this?

We went down two flights of stairs and finally came upon a lounge area. There were another couple of guards there along with two maids who were prepping the tiered tower of sweets along with some tea.

Was he going to poison me? Or was he just playing mind tricks?

We used to have tea all the time when I was learning under him. It was a bitter cold memory that came back to me as he sat down and smiled.

"Just like the good ol' times, right, Cor?"

I took a seat carefully, not sure what to think. All I knew was that I couldn't let my guard down here —not once.

CHAPTER XIV

Zach

Ellie practically burst open the door. Her eyes were wide, and she scanned the room for something. Gabe stepped out of the bathroom in his towel that barely fit around his waist, startled.

"Are you all right, Ellie?" he asked, water dripping down from his dark hair.

She threw him the clothes she had in her hand. "Change quickly. Your father is in town."

Gabe was able to catch the suit but not without half a dozen different emotions spreading across his fact. He finally responded, "How do you know what he looks like?"

"Looks like Byron but wasn't Byron. And he sort of has the same facial structure as you. When you become a bounty hunter, you pick these things up. Could save your life and lead you to your target."

I nodded in agreement. It had come in handy to notice the small things that relatives could share for all the races. The only one we couldn't figure out was Silurians, but we never took a job to assassinate or bring any of them. We weren't going to risk our lives like that.

Gabe stared at the clothes.

Ellie gestured for him to go back into the bathroom and change. "Hurry. I'm not sure how long he's going to be at that café."

"I just— I don't know what to do. Is it a good idea to go see him like this?"

Ellie put her hands on her hips. "If you see him now, you don't have to worry about Byron intercepting the letter. I scanned the area. He isn't here. This might be the easiest way to go talk to him, so go."

"What if he takes me straight to the house? What are you two going to do?"

"If you aren't back by nightfall, and we don't hear from you, we'll find our way in," Ellie said. "Now go."

He nodded and turned to the bathroom and went inside to change. Ellie sat down on the edge of the bed and sighed.

"What is it?" I asked.

She shrugged. "He just looked a lot like Byron. It made all the memories come flooding back. I want to know why all this is happening to us—happening to the world. I just want it to be over."

The thought of Byron made me sick. It also made me sick to know we were close to him and his home. But the others wanted to save Cor and deep down, I knew I didn't want to see him suffer. That didn't mean I wanted to risk our lives to save him though.

"Do you think Gabe's father is key in stopping Byron?"

Another shrug. "We shall see. I don't see many other options for us. I just hope we're able to get Cor out of there. And, of course, not die in the process."

She could say that again. We were risking a lot to go and try to help him. I shifted on the bed and peered up at the ceiling, doing my best to try to not think of what all the stains were and picked out shapes. One of them looked like a squirrel.

"It will be fine. It always is. Cor is good at getting himself out of thought scrapes just like we are."

"I suppose." She let out a breath. "I don't want to be here anymore than you do, but all of this… I just don't know what to do next."

I hated seeing her like this. It made me feel more helpless. "Neither do any of us. I want to turn my back and head for the mountains, but my conscience says otherwise. But I also don't see a way to defeat Byron. He has weaved an impenetrable web. What do we do when the man has convinced everyone he's bringing good to this world? He's already practically taken down, or started to take down, three races. He only has one more to go and then has to clean up any stragglers."

"Exactly. All we have left are the Lyrans, who are at least fierce in battle, but I have no idea what his plan is to take them down. It might not have to do anything with a battle, just like in the Sirian Zone. He could just distract them."

"Perhaps we can find some sort of diary or battle plans when we're in his home. That would make all this more worthwhile."

She shot me a look. "Are you saying saving Cor is not worth it?"

I shrugged. "I'm just saying he wouldn't do the same for us. So perhaps we should add to the list of things we can get out of this plan."

She frowned but didn't say anything for a moment. She knew I was right. He wouldn't have come back for us. He didn't come back for us. Granted, he saved our lives during the attack, but after that, we were on our own.

All this would have been better if he had just stuck around.

I didn't know if that was true, but I wanted to

believe. I wanted to believe in a life better than this one, but with our background, I knew that wouldn't have been the case. Fate led us here for a reason, and no matter what, we would be facing the same things.

"Where would we even search though? The house will be huge. Gabe hasn't ever been there, and I doubt he will come back tonight. Even if he did, he will be followed and we'll have to make a run for it," Ellie commented.

She had a good point. I didn't expect Gabe to come back either. I honestly doubt his father would help him. It was possible but unlikely. Nothing ever went that smoothly for us, and I didn't think that was going to stop now.

Gabe stepped out of the bathroom in his suit with his hair slicked back either naturally or he'd found some gross gel in the bathroom. I doubted he would use someone else's hair gel. He must have had some great hair genes. Byron had some nice hair too, so perhaps it was his from his father's side.

"Well, how do I look?"

Ellie gave him a thumbs-up. "Great. Now let's go."

She stood up and hurried him out the door. She turned to me. "I'll be back in a little bit."

I gave her my own thumbs-up, and the door closed. Silence engulfed me, and I took a deep breath and let it out slowly. This would go fine. It had to. We had come so far. We would all make it out alive. We had to.

It felt like a rock in my stomach. Anytime we started a mission or job, the rock appeared. It was probably not good for me to worry so much, but I couldn't help it—our lives were on the line. At any moment I could lose the last person I cared about.

Now it was a couple of people. Gabe was really nice, and I considered him a friend after everything we had been through. I still didn't know how I felt about Cor. I was mad at him, but we had known each other our whole lives. Could I really come to hate someone who used to mean so much to me? He was a little older than me, and as kids, it felt like so much more. I looked up to him. Even though he got into a lot of trouble, he stood up for me and others. He cared and usually did the right thing or at least what he thought was the right thing. It wasn't as if he didn't break any laws.

But then there was the attack and he disappeared on us. The person I had looked up to for as long as I could remember had turned his back on us. Neither of us was the same after that. Now he was back in our lives, and although we aren't exactly acting like nothing happened, I still felt… weird about it all.

The problem was we didn't have time to process everything that had happened in the past week. We had been attacked, kidnapped, and on the run. Once this was over, perhaps we could talk about it all and mend the relationships.

That is, if we survived what was to come.

CHAPTER XV

Gabe

What was I going to do? What was I going to say?

I knew I shouldn't fret like I was, or at least I shouldn't be fretting over the things I was fretting over. I was worried what he would think of me, not about whether he would help us or if he might be siding with Byron.

What was wrong with me?

There were more important things going on than

for me to worry whether or not my father would be proud of me. Why was I like this? Why did focus on the things that didn't matter?

As I took deep breaths, I felt Ellie's hand squeeze mine. I turned to her, and she smiled.

"It will be all right. Just be yourself and see if he'll help us."

My heart felt as if it had warmed up. Was this what it was like to have friends? Was this what other people experienced while growing up? I never had anyone try to comfort me besides my mother and then, of course, Cor. Or perhaps friends weren't generally this caring and I had lucked out for once in my life.

"Thank you. That means a lot. I just don't know what to say to him. But I'll figure it out. And I'm sure he will help us after he learns about what Byron did to..."

I would have to tell him about my mother if he hadn't already heard. I would tell him what Byron did, and perhaps that would get him to finally do something about this. He loved her, after all. Or, at least, that was what my mother said. She always talked about how father cared about her—cared about us—and would send her random presents and sweet love letters. But he never came to visit after I was born. Why was that? Would I finally learn the truth?

"Okay, this is it." Ellie let go of my hand and nodded to the building. "He's in here. Or at least he was. If you can't find him, just come back to the motel. I'll—"

Without warning, a man stepped out of the café, causing me to fall back. Ellie jumped away, and I didn't see where she went as my eyes were fixed on the person in front of me.

He was tall with blond hair that was slicked back and a well-trimmed mustache that had been curled at the ends. His red suit was made of the finest material, and he had golden buttons and a vest that accented it perfectly. He appeared like Byron, but there was something a little bit different about him. He was a little older with a few more wrinkles.

"Father?" I whispered as he glanced down at me.

His brows furrowed in confusion. "Gabriel?"

All was silent for a moment as we just stared at

each other. I couldn't believe this was happening. My father was standing above me. I finally had come face to face with my father.

I glanced around for Ellie, but she was nowhere to be found. She must have worried Byron was with him and decided to get out of there in case all of this went south. I doubted that would be the case, but it would be better if only I were captured, and she and Zach could figure out how to save Cor and me. So, at the moment, I had to face my father all alone.

My father held out his hand. "Let's get you off the ground."

He was strong. I could tell that by his hand as he helped me up. I needed to work on building up my strength like that. I said a thank you and dusted myself off. For a moment we were silent. I didn't know what to say and it was clear he didn't either, which meant Byron didn't warn him about me. How much did he know about what Byron was up to? Or did he simply ignore everything his brother was doing?

My father spoke first. "What are you doing here?

Why aren't you in the Sirian Zone?"

So he didn't know about the attack. "I… um…"

He shook his head as he glanced around, as if looking for someone. "No, let's head back to the estate. We can talk there."

I felt my heart skip a beat. "Is Uncle Byron there?"

My father furrowed his eyebrows, as if surprised I would ask him that. "Um, I think he got in last night. I haven't really spoken to him. He's in a different wing, and we even go weeks without running into each other when we both are home. Why? Is something a matter?"

I didn't know how to answer that. "I… Let's get back to the house first, and then we'll talk."

He nodded slowly. "Right. I guess we have a lot to talk about. It's… been a while."

He could say that again.

We didn't have much trouble as we headed back to the estate. I expected something to go wrong when we entered the gate, then when we entered the house, then as we walked through the hallways, but nothing ever happened. Now that we were in the lounge area, and I felt as if someone wasn't going to appear and try to kill me, I was able to really appreciate the beauty of his home.

I glanced around, observing the seafoam-green walls with scarlet drapes around each and every window. The natural light coming in was soothing, and no extra lamps were needed. The carpet was a red-and-gold pattern and matched the lounge chairs and sofas that littered the room. We sat at a small table for four people.

Father motioned to the maid and butler who stood at the ready near the door. He handed a sack to the butler who came over.

"Can you bring us some afternoon tea? And use this tea I obtained in town."

The butler nodded and went to the maid who went off to prep the tea. Both of them were humans. The butler was a little older than my father but not by much. He was clean-shaven, had green eyes, and his hair was beginning to go bald in back. The maid, however, was younger—probably about my age. She wore glasses and had red hair that was braided into two pigtails.

I turned to my father. "So, do you normally stay here? I know a lot of the aristocrats in the Human Zone like to visit the cities from time to time."

"I used to visit every once in a while, but lately I've been staying here. There is a lot to do in this house, and I have guests over quite frequently, so I'm never bored. But I do like to shop for new suits and hats in the city since the tailors here aren't as great."

That made me smile a bit. Perhaps my enjoying hats was genetic. Some reason that made me feel a little bit closer to him.

It wasn't long before the maid came back and set down the tray of sweets and savories along with the tea.

"One lump or two, sir? And would you like milk?" she asked me.

"I… um… two sugars and milk please."

She nodded as she prepped my cup and then prepped my father's without needing to ask. I assumed he drank more than his weight in tea just like Byron did. The maid poured the tea, which came out in a dark amber. I smelled the soft scent of orange blossoms. If I wasn't mistaken, it was bergamot.

The maid finished up and bowed. "Will that be all, sir?"

My father nodded. "Yes, now leave us."

The maid bowed and followed the butler out of the room. My father took his teaspoon and stirred his tea gently.

"So," he began as he took a small finger sandwich from the platter. "What brings you to the Human Zone? I didn't think Lili would ever let you leave. It was why you never came to stay with me when you were younger."

Was that true? Did my mother not allow me to leave the Sirian Zone? It didn't matter now. I peered down at my tea and the small lemon tart I had grabbed. Now nothing seemed appetizing. "She's... I..."

I tried pushing back the tears, but they came out in a fury. I wasn't exactly sobbing. It was as if my body didn't know what to do except cry. I sat there, quiet, as I wiped my face with my napkins.

My father watched me. "Did something happen?"

"She was murdered. I watched her die."

I couldn't read the expression on his face. He didn't seem genuinely surprised but more sorrowful —as if he knew it was going to happen. Did he know she was in danger? If so, why didn't he stop it?

"Tell me what happened."

I went through everything that had happened the past week—from the attack on Zynon to my mother's death and being arrested. I told him everything Byron had done and the things he told me about my great-grandfather and how he had wanted to destroy all the other races. My father was quiet and expressionless through it all. He waited until I finished everything before he commented.

"I knew my brother wanted to fulfill our grandfather's dreams, but I never could imagine he would take it this far. You said you had two friends that you are traveling with?"

I nodded, wiping away what I hoped were the last tears.

“Where are they now?”

I hesitated. Should I tell him? Did he want to help us, or was he just gathering information for Byron? So far he hadn’t reacted to anything I had said, but he didn’t seem like he was in on any of it. It was clear I was still with them, so it wasn’t like he couldn’t just search the entire town for them. For that matter, Byron could find out from the staff that I was here and then go searching for them.

“They are at the motel off Main Street. Near where I ran into you.”

He nodded. “I’ll send for them and get them in here. Then, from there, we can figure out what to do next.”

“I don’t know if they are going to exactly come in willingly. I mean, they were pretty suspicious people, for good reason of course.”

“Don’t worry. I’ll get them here. I’ll explain it all. Besides, they were more than likely going to sneak in here to help your friend Cor, weren’t they? You were just the distraction?”

I hesitated. How did he figure that out? “I guess an invitation could work. But Byron can’t know about it.”

"Of course. Let me get my guards, and they'll go have a talk with them.”

"Perhaps I could go—”

"No. I will not risk Byron getting to you. You are safer where I can see you. My guards can handle it.”

I nodded, not sure how this all was going to play out. I prayed they would listen and not just attack them.

CHAPTER XVI

Ellie

I thought Gabe's father was going to spot me as I jumped back, but his eyes didn't seem to move from Gabe's.

It probably didn't matter—he probably didn't know who I was, and I was overreacting. But with everything that had happened, I couldn't be too sure. Byron was a sneaky bastard, and I wouldn't put it pass him to use his own brother. There was also the fact that they looked alike that had me worried.

What if he was working for Byron? What if this was going to be a big mistake?

There was no going back now. Gabe was going to tell his father what was going on, and we had to hope for the best. I hurried off through the alleyway and made my way back to the motel room. Zach would be wondering where I was, and we would need to plan how we were going to sneak into the estate later tonight.

It might be wise for us to stake it out before then. I would bring it up with Zach. It wasn't as if we had anything else to do other than take a shower. That was the first thing I definitely needed to do.

I kept my eyes out for anyone suspicious. So far, it was all clear. I hated it. It made me feel even less safe. There was always someone after us, whether it was Byron or some other people made at us for one of our jobs. Or because I got in a fight with them last time I was here. However, I couldn't remember the last time I was in this town and it was clear no one was looking for us, which made me even more worried.

It was because I didn't know what to expect. When someone was following, I knew they were going to confront me. With Wanted signs, I knew someone was going to try to turn me in. With guns pointed at me, I knew they were going to shoot and ask questions later. But with nothing, what was I going to expect? Because if I knew anything it was that no obvious threat did not ever mean everything was fine. More often than not, it meant something terrible was going to happen.

I made it back to the motel, and Zach was still lying on the bed, staring up at the ceiling. To distract himself, he usually tried to find shapes and figures in ceilings, clouds, whatever he could see. I found it passed the time as well, but it never helped me calm down like it did him.

He leaned up on his elbows. "So, was it him?"

I nodded. "Yup. It was his father. Gabe is talking to him now."

"Do you think he'll take him back to the estate?"

I shrugged. "I would guess so. His father looked genuinely surprised to see him. He didn't seem to look like he was going to do anything to hurt him either, so I think we're in the clear. Or at least in the clear to get him in. We'll need to find our own way in."

Zach nodded. "Step one done then."

"Yep." I stretched. "My turn to take a shower. Then we can go out and stake out the area. We need to figure out how many guards there are and see if we can get a grasp the layout somehow."

"How are we going to do that from the outside?"

I shrugged. "A lot of those homes look alike. I think we'll be able to get the general layout. It's not as if we haven't been in a mansion before."

"Ugh, don't remind me."

I chuckled as I went into the bathroom and ran the water. After a few moments, the brownish liquid turned clear, and I stripped and stepped inside.

I felt a lot better after cleaning up. We still needed to wash our clothes, but we would do that after we checked out the mansion. We didn't want to waste any daylight.

Zach and I left the motel room and locked the door. I double-checked it even though I knew if someone wanted to get in, they would. At least thieves didn't have anything to steal other than Gabe's old clothes and whatever furniture the place already had. We headed off in the direction of the estates.

"Do you know which one it is?" Zach asked as we headed toward the hillside.

I let out a breath. "No, but don't aristocrats like to put their name in big letters at the gates?"

"True, you have a point there."

We walked, careful to keep an eye for any guards or Byron himself. I kept my hand on my revolver the entire time we moved forward. It was quiet, and there was quite a nice afternoon breeze compared to heat we had traveled here in. I could see why some people would want to live out here. The hills were covered in trees and flowers that were in bloom. I saw yellows, whites, pinks, and purples color the hillside. The air was sweet, even over the smell that was coming off our clothes. We really needed to wash them.

As we turned a corner, I heard a carriage coming up from behind us.

"Quick." I grabbed Zach's wrist. "Let's hide behind those trees."

We jumped behind the trees just as a carriage with two horses came around the corner. As I peered around the tree, I saw a familiar blond-haired man.

It was Byron.

My heart began to race. That was a close one. If he had spotted us, we would have been goners. And he would have rubbed it in our faces how easy it was to find us. I would have felt humiliated.

"Should we follow him? See what house he goes to?" Zach asked.

I pointed at him. "Good idea. Let's keep an eye on it, but I didn't want to be that close just in case."

"Of course. We can stay a ways behind and see where he goes."

After the carriage was far enough away, we jumped back out, but stayed near the tree line so we didn't stand out as much. Out to the side like this we appeared like two people out for a walk and not as if we were following. Or, at least, that was what I hoped.

The carriage wasn't moving too fast, so it was easy to keep an eye on them. We watched as it turned on a pathway that led up to a mansion on the hill. Both Zach and I stopped and peered at the area he headed toward.

"So do you think that is it?" I asked.

He nodded. "I think it is. Should we get closer and see if we can tell how many guards there are?"

I took a breath. I had a feeling it was going to be a lot, but there was only one way to find out. "Yeah, let's."

After the carriage was long gone and we didn't have to worry about Byron spotting us, we headed up the pathway. It was a bit of a trek, as we had to venture over a hill, but nothing we weren't used to. We definitely had stayed fit over the years.

We got to the top of the hill, and I gasped at what lay before me.

First of all, the house was huge. Calling it a mansion was an understatement. It was practically a castle. It had appeared much smaller from below.

It was going to take forever to figure out where Cor was. He could be anywhere.

I took some calm, deep breaths. We would figure this out. We needed to focus.

Scanning around, I found a ton of guards. I couldn't believe how Byron had hired. Just how rich was this family? It made sense he would have so many people—especially after the stunts he had pulled in the past couple of weeks. Anyone who knew the truth of what he had done would want his head on a silver platter.

I wondered how high-tech his place was. I peered around but didn't see any sort of machine I recognized. It took a lot of upkeep to use technology all the way out here. Perhaps that was why he had so many guards. It was probably cheaper than all that.

So going through the front door was going to be impossible. And the back door. The best odds were to find a carriage and sneak in that way. Or, perhaps, if any of these guards left the area, we could knock them out and steal their uniform.

I bit my lip. That actually might work.

I studied the building once more and noticed something off about the windows on the top floor. They all had bars on the west wing. It was like some sort of prison.

That was where Cor was. It had to be.

CHAPTER XVII

Cor

Tea with Byron wasn't the worst thing in the world, but it had been up there. The food was good, and the tea was heavenly, I would give him that, but I spent most of the time wondering if he was going to poison me. I watched as he picked stuff off the plate, but it was clear the food hadn't been laced. I wouldn't let my guard down, however. That was probably what he wanted. And then he would try something, just like he always did.

Byron talked about what life was like before he betrayed me. He reminded me all that he taught me and how many hours he had spent as my tutor. With each memory he brought up, it felt like I was reliving the tragedy over and over again. It reminded me of the life I wanted to provide for Ellie—it reminded me of the life that we lost because this asshole wanted to destroy everyone I cared about. He had led me to believe that he cared, only to destroy everything in the end.

I wanted more than anything to watch him suffer.

After we finished eating, I had noticed that I nearly destroyed the cloth napkin that I was given as I had wrung it in my hands each time he spoke. I didn't feel bad, as they could easily replace it. He had the money. I could have made a scene and thrown things against the wall and whatnot, but I also didn't want to receive any punishment that he or the guards might give me. No, I would play nicely until I figured a way out of there.

Because it wasn't as if anyone would come and get me.

Byron had made that perfectly clear. He told me that he sent men into the woods to look for Ellie and the others, but they were long gone by the time they started the search. They could be anywhere on Mu. They had mentioned they were going to head for the mountains, and that was probably what they had done. There was no way they didn't leave me behind—they would be too stupid to risk their lives to save me. No, we knew going into this that not all of us would get out of it alive. I deserved to be the one killed by Byron after what I had done.

There was no way they could save me from this place either. There were too many guards—it would be impossible. Although we had been in quite a few impossible scenarios in the past week, this would be too much even for Ellie. She wouldn't be that stupid to risk it all for me. Maybe at one time, but not after I betrayed her.

I didn't deserve them coming for me.

It was why I didn't ask for their help after Kaus was destroyed. I didn't deserve it—I deserved to be alone. I had to fix it all out on my own.

Or, perhaps, I was afraid of her choosing to turn

her back on me. Perhaps I figured if I left then I couldn't find out if she would truly leave me. Now I knew the truth—now I knew if things got hard, it was ever man for themselves. I should have figured with everything that happened that would be the case. But part of me had hope she would risk everything for me. Then again, would I have risked everything for her? Did I possess that kind of selflessness any longer?

I glanced down at the courtyard again. The number of guards had not dwindled. I let out a sigh. At least the room was nice and could let in some fresh air. It could definitely be a lot worse. It wasn't as if I was being locked in some madman's house. Oh wait…

As I peered outside, I noticed a carriage coming into the estate. It appeared like the one that Byron had brought me in, so I figured it was him. He said he had some business to take care of after we were done, and I could only imagine what that was. It must have been short since he wasn't gone that long. I watched as the driver brought him to the front of the house, and he jumped down to open the door for him. Byron stepped out.

I turned away. I didn't want to see his face. He made me so angry that I could barely handle it. I had hated Krax with a passion, but this was completely different. Byron had completely betrayed me. He had tricked me and used me, and now I had to live with the fact that I had been deceived.

And I was the reason my people were gone.

I couldn't live with this guilt forever. I needed to make it right—I needed to take him down once and for all. I paced back and forth in the room. How was I going to do that, however? How was I going to get the revenge that not only I wanted but every person in Kaus? All those who had died that day?

I would need help, but I didn't know where Gabe or the others were and if they would even help me. It would be a suicide mission, I was sure, and killing him could potentially make things worse for the world. How he claimed he had set up everything, it would make him look like a martyr. I didn't want that, but I also didn't want him to breathe another breath.

Would they help me kill him if it meant also the destruction of so many people? A war that could potentially end everything?

I collapsed in the middle of the floor. The hard wood felt cold against my skin. None of this was fair. Killing him should end everything, but it didn't. Killing him should bring everyone back, but it didn't. It wasn't fair—he had killed all my people and was labeled a hero. If I killed him, I would be labeled the villain. How was that fair? Why was this world so cruel?

It made me not care about saving everyone and made me want to just go ahead and murder him. But I didn't want anyone to go through what we had. I didn't want anyone else to know the feeling of watching your home destroyed. No, I had to save them from that—I had to save everyone from that.

The door locks clicked, and I heard them open. I expected Byron to be standing there even though I had just seen him enter the house, but it wasn't him. It was another man who appeared similar to Byron. He was a little older, but they were definitely related. I stared at him as I got up.

He stepped inside the cell, but the guards kept the door open. They knew it would be impossible for me to escape, but I could take a hostage. I glanced around but didn't have anything I could use as a weapon. Maybe the sheets.

"What do you want?" I asked. "Who are you?"

"I just came to talk."

"About what?" I asked. "About how Byron is going to destroy the world with his crazy-ass plan? I mean, if you care about anything in this world, then you should do what you can to stop him."

He chuckled. "Yes, Byron is a bit crazy. He's way too forward in how he goes about his plans. It will be his downfall, honestly."

I wasn't sure if I liked where that was heading. "Well, hopefully I get to witness his downfall."

"Don't worry. I believe you will. If you do exactly what I ask of you."

I narrowed my eyes. "What do you mean? Who are you?"

"I'm his brother. I guess technically I'm your boyfriend's father as well. I'm Jonathan Pickett. Gabe told me who you were and that you were being held captive by my brother. I thought I would come see if it was true. Appears it is."

Well, that was a plot twist. This was not how I expected to meet Gabe's father. "So Gabe is here."

"Indeed he is. And I have sent for the other two to be picked up and delivered to me. Then, together, we can take down Byron once and for all."

I watched him closely. He seemed genuine. He really did want to stop his brother. He would have no reason to come up here and tell me this if he was after Gabe and the others. He had to be speaking the truth.

"What do you have in mind?"

CHAPTER XVIII

Zach

So we were going to stake this place out until some guards left, and we stole their clothes. Great.

Ellie and I were sitting in the tree line, watching and waiting. At least in the shade it was pretty decent, and I did enjoy hearing the birds in the afternoon chirp away. I was sitting in a patch of clover and searched around but had only found three-leaf clovers thus far.

"What if they don't leave the estate? They probably live there—look how big it is," I commented as I ran my hands through another chunk of clover. I still didn't spot any four-leaf clovers.

"Someone will probably leave. They have to in order for this to work."

I glanced up and found Ellie still staring at the gate. I let out a sigh.

"Would you leave this beautiful place to go to the town? It's not the best of towns. I mean, look at the motel we're staying at."

"The tailor was nice, and Gabe's father was shopping at some café. It's quaint but not bad. Better than what we had growing up. Besides, there is always a bar to unwind at in the evening."

That was fair. But again, an estate like the one before us probably had everything anyone could wish for, even a bar. That is, if Byron and his brother let the guards and staff use the facilities. Or perhaps they had their own smaller building. That seemed unnecessary though, but men like Byron usually made unnecessary things.

"What will we do once we're in?" I asked, picking at the dandelions now. I had given up on the clovers—there weren't going to be any lucky ones.

She let out a breath. "Well, we figure out where Cor is, but I have a feeling he's on that top floor somewhere. Then we locate Byron's office and see if we can find out what his next course of action is. Then perhaps we can stop it and convince others what's going on."

That was a scenario that would have to go according to plan, and both of us knew that nothing ever went according to plan. Although it would be great if we were able to find his study, break into his desk, find something he might not even have written down, and then escape without a hitch, the odds of all that working were slim. There was also the fact that the longer we were in that castle-mansion place, the more likely we would be caught. Did we risk our lives for information that might not even be there?

Then there was the whole fact that we needed to find and extract Cor, because apparently that was a thing. He wouldn't have risked his life for us, so I wasn't exactly sure why we were risking our lives for him. Ellie had said it was because we were also trying to get information, but I knew that was just an excuse. She would, and has, gone to the ends of the world for him, and that would never change. I needed to accept she was blinded by love and just pray that we would make it out alive.

Not only that, but we also had to home that Gabe was fine and that his dad would help us. If he did, then perhaps all this was possible. If not…well… then we were in for quite the mission.

"I wonder how Gabe is doing," I commented. "And if his father will help us."

"I hope so. Or I at least hope he doesn't tell Byron about him. It was a big risk, but I think it was worth taking. So far there hadn't been any inclination that he is helping Byron, but there is also the fact he hasn't tried to stop him either. That's what worries me the most. He could just be passive about it all because he is loyal to his family or some bogus thing like that."

"Do you think we should wait for him back at the

motel? I mean, he could have come back for us to sneak us in with his father."

Ellie frowned. "I guess that is a possibility, but I think Gabe would be smart enough to not let anyone know about our location. Then again, he might think his dad is innocent. He is a little too trusting at times."

"You don't think his dad is innocent?" I asked, picking a few more dandelions.

"I don't think anyone is innocent until proven otherwise. We have been tricked one too many times, Zach. We have to keep our guard up, or we'll be killed."

"Like when we kept a guard up when we went into that pub a couple of days ago?" I asked, trying to bring a little humor to the conversation.

She sighed. "We were tired and stupid. It won't happen again."

"This place seems like we should have to be on guard all the time, yet I haven't seen anyone looking for us or any posters up. What do you think Byron is planning?"

Ellie shook her head. "I have no idea. He's

sinister and devious. I'm not sure what to think. I want to assume he has some plan for us, but what if he really thought we wouldn't come for Cor and is searching for us elsewhere? We might have an advantage. But, at the same time, I don't believe he's that stupid. I just… I don't know what is going on, and I don't know how to prepare for it."

She had a point there. Usually when we were facing someone who wanted to kill us, they were very clear about how they wanted to kill us. We didn't have to try this hard to understand their intentions since it was always clear. We knew people would send men after us—we knew to always look over our shoulders—but in this case, we didn't know where to look. It felt as if he could come from any direction, and then when he wasn't there, he appears on the other side of us. It just wasn't fair.

Ellie went on. "I also don't want to spend too much time in there. We need to grab the others and get out of here. But we also need to see if Gabe's father will help us. And we need those plans. I don't want the two of us to split up since that never seems to work, especially in places as heavily guarded as this, but I'm not sure if we have any other options at this point."

"If we can even get in," I added. "It's been over an hour, and so far no one has left the premises. We don't know how long shifts will be, and we don't know if the guards will even leave. Maybe we should go back to the motel and hope Gabe comes back."

Ellie shook her head. "No, even if he comes back, it could be a setup. We should wait here and see if we can either attack a guard, spot Cor or Gabe, or find another way in. Besides, if Gabe goes to see us, we'll see him leave from here. This is the best spot."

"If he's even in the castle. I mean, we know he's with his father, but maybe they didn't leave the town."

Ellie bit her lip. She knew I was right. "If that were the case, he would have brought him back to us before I was done getting ready. More than likely, Gabe is in there talking to him now."

"And Byron?"

"And Byron is in there. Hopefully he doesn't find out about Gabe. It's a big place. If Gabe convinced his father Byron was evil and his father didn't have anything to do with the plans, then he won't let Byron know about Gabe."

That was even more wishing. Although the place was big and I had a feeling Byron and his brother didn't see eye to eye—not after he had a relationship with a Sirian. But they both owned this place, so they kept that much peace.

"So what do we do now?" I asked.

"We wait. You know how to wait. We're used to staking out places."

I sighed. I really didn't want to stay here, knowing full well that the odds of anyone leaving were slim. "Fine, but we're definitely getting food later."

"That all depends on how fast we need to get out of here."

My stomach grumbled at the thought of food. I knew I should have brought a snack. I had hoped we would go back to the motel before doing anything drastic. I should have known better.

It felt like another hour had passed, and no one came out of the gates. We watched as some carriages went by to take people to the other homes around this area, but none were for Byron's home. I had moved a little bit to search for a four-leaf clover, but even after a couple of hours, I hadn't found a single one.

Finally, after another half an hour, I found one. I smiled as I picked it and lifted it up.

"I did it! Our luck is about to change!"

And at that moment, there was movement all around us and suddenly someone placed a dark bag over my head.

CHAPTER XIX

Gabe

My father had sent men to bring Ellie and Zach here. I paced around my room, waiting for them to arrive, knowing full well they were going to put up a fight. They weren't people who trusted, well, at all. I wished my father let me go back and talk to them, although I knew they would still be hesitant. They trusted me, but they would think it a trap, and the way my father was retrieving them more than likely led them to believe he was going to turn them in to Byron.

I let out a sigh. This couldn't ever be easy, but once they were here and my father explained everything and put together his plan, then we could take down Byron once and for all. I couldn't wait. I wanted more than anything to see that man taken down.

I paced around my room, waiting for someone to retrieve me. My room. It was strange to think my father had a room already made for me. Apparently he wanted me to live with him at some point in my life. My mother had never told me—never gave me the option. Would life had been better if I had grown up here? Or would Byron still have tried to torture me? He had spent so much time in the Sirian Zone—why didn't my father ever visit?

I had always thought he had been ashamed of me, mainly because that's what Byron had told me. But that wasn't what happened—that was clear with this room.

As I stepped around, I found photos from every achievement and point in my life. There were many photos I had taken with my mother, which made my heart ache. I felt a bit better after the sobbing earlier, but there was still an emptiness inside that I didn't believe would ever go away. Perhaps it would fade in time, but I had a feeling that emptiness would linger.

Besides photos, there were some of my favorite things. There were posters of the ocean, some stuffed whales and starfish, and the room was themed in a beautiful green. How did he know all these things about me? Was it just coincidence, or had my mother told him?

I picked up the whale and gave it a squeeze. It was soft and cuddly. I wondered if I could take him with me or if we were going to be able to stay here.

I knew the odds of that were slim, but that didn't mean I didn't want to dream. What would my life have been like if my parents had stayed together? Would we have been happy? Would we have stopped Byron already?

Something inside me said that wasn't the case and that perhaps my father didn't stay around because of him. I collapsed on the bed, wishing all my questions could be answered at that moment, but I knew they wouldn't be.

After a few moments, I heard a knock at the door. I got up and opened it to find my father and a familiar face.

"Cor!"

I rushed to him and wrapped my arms around him. He kissed the side of my head and wrapped his arms around me.

"What are you doing here?" Cor asked. "Why didn't you make a break for it when you had a chance?"

I peered over at my father. "I… I figured this was our only chance to stop Byron. If my father was on our side, then we could do it…"

Cor glanced at my father but didn't say anything. My father gestured into the room. "Let's talk a bit about what we're going to do next."

All three of us went into my room, and I took a seat on my bed. Cor sat next to me, and my father grabbed a chair from the little nook he had made me by the window. Cor grabbed my hand and squeezed it.

"Byron is out of control. I had heard about the attack on Zynon and had my suspicion, but after hearing what happened in the Sirian Zone"—he took a deep breath—"I can't sit by and let what is happening continue."

"He destroyed my people," Cor interjected. "Why didn't you stop him then?"

My father was silent for a moment, as if trying to gather himself. "I… I don't have a good response to that. I know the Kausians used to be accepted by everyone at one time and that my grandfather caused them to retreat to their zone and convince everyone that you all were not to be trusted. Part of me wanted to believe that he hadn't done that and it was a misunderstanding. I didn't know what to do when your home was attacked. I thought that would be the end of it, honestly. I didn't think my brother would continue all this."

I glanced at Cor, who was still frowning. It was clear that he didn't believe him. I turned back to my father. "How are we going to stop him?"

"Well, first we need to find what he's going to do next. We need proof to show the people."

"And why can't you find that? He's your brother after all."

My father studied Cor closely. "He doesn't trust me. He has guards on the lookout, making sure I don't go into his wing. But with you two and your other friends, I think we'll be able to find it."

"Ellie and Zach are here as well?" Cor asked.

"Not exactly, but I sent my men to retrieve them."

Cor laughed. "Good luck with that. Ellie trusts people less than I do. You will be lucky if your men survive the encounter."

Father hesitated. "I think they'll be all right. I just sent them to the motel. If there is any trouble, they'll let them know."

I had to agree with Cor—there was no way this was going to go well. We both knew how Ellie could be. She didn't trust anyone, and rightly so. She had been through a lot, and that sort of survival didn't come easy. Hopefully no one got hurt and the guards would be able to explain everything in a way that led her to trust them. I doubted it though, as Byron was here and he was always running amok. I just had to hope they convinced her somehow.

"Now," my father began as he leaned back. "How did the two of you meet?"

I felt my cheeks grow warm. There was no way I was going to talk about my love life with my father whom I hadn't talked to about anything before. I didn't even know how to answer that question. I fumbled with my hands as Cor squeezed my shoulder.

"He saved me." Cor smiled. "I got in a bit of trouble with some gangsters and was left out in the middle of the desert all by my lonesome, and he came along and helped me get back to the nearest town. If it weren't for him, I'd be some vulture's dinner. That was two years ago, and we have been together ever since."

Father glanced between us with his light blue eyes. The more I was with him, the more I noticed the similarities between him and Byron. It was unnerving, but it was clear they were not the same person. He was kind and wanted to hear about my life, whereas Byron always told me how awful I was and that I needed to die. I couldn't imagine Byron doing that.

"Your mother said you were on the surface for the past two years. You really worried her. What did you do to survive?"

I could feel Cor stiffen up, just as I did. I looked away. "Oh, you know, different jobs here and there."

"It was a team effort. But we almost got Gabe introduced into the society, but then Byron messed that all up," Cor added.

"Right. The society. I hated those people and never went to functions. Every once in a while Byron would bring them to meet here and I would have to help entertain, but that was about it for how much I talked to them. They do not think about society as a whole or about what effects their businesses cause to the lower classes."

He definitely didn't sound like Byron. The more I heard my father talk, the more I wished he had been in my life as a child.

"If you really think that, why didn't you stop your brother earlier? And why did you leave Gabe on his own?" Cor asked.

I elbowed him, but he didn't budge. It was clear he didn't trust my father like I had.

My father stood up and walked over to the window. "It's true. I should have stopped my brother earlier, but I really… I didn't think he would take it this far. Our grandfather was a horrible, crazy man. I didn't actually think he believed all of what he said. As for not being there when Gabriel was younger… I have no excuse. Your mother and I weren't exactly married, not to mention she was a queen who had to raise an heir to the throne. I had hoped if I wasn't there that people wouldn't be so harsh to Gabriel. Apparently I was wrong, and I'm truly sorry for that. I just pray that your sister will be able to bring peace after everything that has happened."

I peered down at my hands as Cor kept me close. Kishiko was all on her own. I wished I could be there for her. I wished I would be able to tell her it would all be okay. But I knew the only way to help her was to take Byron down. At least she knew the truth—at least she knew her brother wasn't a murderer. I just prayed the others didn't twist her memories of what happened that night.

Father turned back to us. "Once the guards bring your friends, then we can speak of my plan. Until then, I think we should take you back to where he's keeping you, Cor. I just wanted a chance to talk to the both of you."

Cor turned to me and gave me a kiss. "I'll be back soon. Don't worry about me. The room is rather nice, all things considering."

With that, they both left me in what was supposed to be my room. I glanced around, still not sure what to make of any of it. I took a deep breath and leaned back onto my bed. It almost felt as if all of this was simply a dream and I would wake up at any moment now.

But what would be awaiting me when I woke up and realized the truth?

CHAPTER XX

Ellie

Well, shit.

The bag was over my head before I could react. It was no matter. I knew where Zach was, so I could easily fight back without hurting him. Probably.

I pulled out my knife and swung it around. I felt it hit something, and a man yelped. As I kept swinging it back and forth, I sensed the others jump back as I no longer had anyone trying to grab me. I pulled the cloth bag off my head and faced my attackers.

Zach was already cuffed. He did not have as good of reflexes as I did. I counted the men who surrounded us. A dozen at least. Fuck.

As I reached for my gun, the men all pulled out their own guns and aimed them at me. I realized in that moment they hadn't been ready to shoot, which meant they wanted us to come alive. That made sense since Byron wanted to torture us.

"Put your weapons down. We aren't going to hurt you, but if you try anything, we'll retaliate," one of the men said.

I sighed as I lowered my weapon. There was no way I was getting out of this, not to mention they already had Zach. I wouldn't be able to guarantee his safety if this turned into a shoot-out. I watched as the guard leaned down and grabbed my weapons.

"Search her—she might have more."

Damn, they were smart. I did, in fact, have more weapons. One couldn't be too careful when dealing with, well, anyone. I had been in way too many incidents where if I hadn't brought more than my fair share of weapons, I would have been dead.

Men came up to me on both sides and took my weapons. I sighed as they frisked me, appropriately, and took everything I had.

The man, who clearly was in charge, motioned to the others. "Put the hood back on. We can't let anyone know who we're bringing in. And bind her hands."

I laughed. "I mean, it's obvious, isn't it? There're not many women who wear the clothes that I do."

The head guard didn't say anything, but Zach laughed. "She also doesn't shut up, so everyone hears her voice. Better gag her as well."

"Zach, I swear when this is over…"

"I'm joking. Please don't gag her. She doesn't ever give empty threats."

I expected the guards to tell us to shut up like they normally did, but they didn't say anything. They simply shoved us forward toward where I figured the house was.

Something didn't add up.

We had been surrounded and attacked many times through the years, and every time we were attacked, no one was ever this kind. Especially if I managed to injure one of them. It usually resulted in some kicking, punching, and so forth. Not a kind *come with us* sort of deal. I expected more retaliation.

Which meant they were ordered to not hurt us, but I had already figured that out. Even if that were the case, usually when I backtalked a guard or put up a fight, they gave me some kind of kick or punch. Byron didn't want us dead, but since the guards were told all his lies and also hated us, they usually gave us some grief. These men seemed like they were just following orders and we were almost treated like…guests?

But who in the right mind would capture guests like this?

It had to be Byron. He was probably playing mind games with us again. I wouldn't fall for it—I wouldn't go willingly like this. If they were ordered to behave, then that meant it would be less of an issue trying to get away.

The problem was, I couldn't see. And they took my weapons. And they bound my hands. It might be better to get into the estate this way since they clearly were already looking for us. Besides, I had a couple of bobby pins hidden in my hair to help pick a lock. We should be fine.

That is, if they were taking us there and this wasn't some other person who had been after us. That was definitely possible. Did I ask them? Would they even tell me the truth? Or did I just go along with it all and figure it out once I got there?

If the past told me anything, it was that I never got the information I wanted from guards like this. It was better we waited, especially since they weren't hurting us at the moment. I let them lead me to wherever we were going. I heard a gate swing open and knew it had to be Byron's house. That or some other rich person near here. Either way, we hadn't walked all the way to town, and it was more than likely Byron since he was the one who was after us.

So we would have to all break out. At least Gabe was already on the inside and could try to free us.

Then a thought hit me—what if it was Gabe's father who had sent for us? If that were the case, why didn't they say so? But that would have made sense for why they were being nice to us—it just didn't make sense why they didn't say anything. Either way, we were being led into the home and one of the two men was waiting for us. I hoped it was Gabe's father even if this was all a strange way to pick us up.

We zigzagged through the corridors. I didn't hear anyone talking, which was strange. After a bit, we were forced up some stairs, and I did my best not to trip. The man pushing me was quite skilled in leading people upstairs. I had many guards try, and usually it caused me to fumble. Granted, not many buildings had stairs—at least not in the Human, Lyran, or Kaus Zones. The Sirian Zone had a lot of stairs, and I had heard the Silurian Zone had a lot, although not many people outside the Silurians were allowed in there, so I wouldn't know from experience.

We finally stopped, and I heard a door open. I was shoved inside the room, and one of the men finally took off my mask.

And I was standing inside a bedroom. I glanced around, confused and a bit disoriented. Zach appeared as equally perplexed. The room was nice —definitely not a cell.

I turned to say something when the door shut. I tried the doorknob, but it was locked.

"So, who do you think brought us here?" Zach asked.

I shrugged. "At this point in time, I do not know." I went over to the bed and found a note.

PLEASE CHANGE INTO SOMETHING MORE SUITABLE. THERE ARE CLOTHES IN THE CLOSET.

There was no signature. I sighed, knowing full well what was going to be in there. I opened the closet and found suits for Zach and some simple dresses for me. I cursed under my breath.

"What is it?" Zach asked as he stepped up to the closet. He laughed. "Oh, I see. They want to dress you up nice and purdy."

I gave him a look. "You know how disgusting it feels to have your captive want you to dress up for him?"

"Hey, he's making me dress up as well."

"Not the same."

"It's kind of the same. It's not like any of these dresses show much skin. If they were all skimpy, then I would agree with you."

He had a point there. These dresses were just something to blend in with—not to play dress up with like that other time. I sighed as I grabbed the smallest suit, praying it would fit.

"Hey, that's mine."

"This size is too small for you, but it might fit me. Whoever is our captive doesn't know our sizes, which makes me believe that it might have been Gabe's dad, not Byron, who brought us in. He has never met us."

Zach nodded. "Yeah, I was wondering why they didn't retaliate after you stabbed that guy. But Byron does like to play mind games, so who knows what he might do just to keep our guard down?"

"That is definitely true. I wouldn't put it past

Byron to make us relaxed so we reveal that Gabe is with his father. And to put a wrench in our plans to help Cor."

"Right. Cor."

I rolled my eyes. "What is it, Zach? You have been acting really weird about him. He was your best friend at one point."

"Yeah, and then he betrayed us and we went hunting for him to make him pay. Now you are head over heels for him again, and it's just odd, okay? You hated him so much. You are acting like a school girl."

"I'm not acting like a schoolgirl."

"Yes, you are! And he's taken and you are still letting yourself believe you will have your happily-ever-after. What do you think will happen when this is done?"

I let out a breath and shook my head. "I don't want to talk about this right now Zach. We need to focus."

"See, this is why you two are great for each other. You ignore your emotions and find excuses."

"I think trying to save the world is a pretty good

excuse to push back personal problems."

He grabbed one of the suits and headed toward the bathroom. "If you say so. I think it's just going to get in the way, but we shall see."

Zach closed the door, and I shook my head. I had no idea what his problem was. I quickly got out my clothes and put on the smallest size that was provided for us. It was a little big but not in the length of the trousers, and they didn't feel like they were going to fall down, which was all I needed. Just as I finished adjusting my suspenders, there was a knock at the door.

I reached for my gun and realized I was unarmed. I couldn't do anything but wait to see who it was. In stepped a blond, and it took me a second to realize it was not Byron but in fact Gabe's father.

"Hello. I'm Jonathan Pickett. I believe you know my son."

CHAPTER XXI

Cor

I didn't like this. I didn't like this one bit.

Sure, it was nice having someone, anyone really, help us against Byron, but something didn't feel right about it. He was too… nice. Gabe's father acted like he cared, and yet he didn't appear to have even lifted a finger to help save, well, anyone thus far. So why was he sticking his neck out now?

It could be because of Gabe, or it could be

because he wants something else. As to what that something was, however, I had no idea. If he was helping Byron, he wouldn't have taken me to see Gabe. He could have easily persuaded Gabe without me since, well, Gabe was far more trusting than most. There was no clear motive I could see under everything. He appeared to want his brother gone and to stop all this madness. But, again, why hadn't he done anything up to this point?

Had it really just been his son who made him stand up for what was right? Or perhaps hearing about the death of the one he loved pushed him forward. Personally, after hearing about the destruction of an entire civilization, I would have tried to stop all the madness, but perhaps I was just soft.

He also didn't seem to mind that Gabe was involved with a Kausian. That surprised me. Then again, he had fallen in love with someone not of the same race. Perhaps it made him feel connected to his son. Or perhaps he thought it was just a fling and wasn't going to worry about it at the moment.

He wouldn't like me if he knew all the things I

had done to survive, however. Or, at least, wouldn't want me for his son.

It didn't bother me that I had slept with men and women for money. I never cared who knew and didn't feel ashamed of it, especially since it was the only work someone like me could find besides bounty hunting, which I did as well. It just bothered me that it wasn't always accepted. I felt ashamed even though I knew I shouldn't. I also didn't want Ellie to find out the truth. I had promised myself to her and then…

Well, the rest was history. Once she'd found out about it, I couldn't let her know I felt as if I had betrayed her by sleeping with others and moving on with Gabe. I had to act like it was no big deal even though it was in my mind—or, at least, it was in some ways. The act of being a prostitute wasn't what bothered me but the fact I promised her the best future and everything had been ruined because I had trusted the wrong person. Then what was supposed to be ours was no longer ours—it was just a way of life. Then my heart, which was also supposed to be hers, was no longer just hers. It was also Gabe's.

But that didn't mean I didn't love her any less, it just… I didn't know anymore. I ran my hands through my hair. It didn't matter. There was no way any of this was going to work. Byron was too smart even if we had Gabe's father on our side. He had told me he didn't care if he died. He said that he would appear like a martyr and that people would want revenge and take action against the other nations. We were doomed.

So I didn't have to worry about Gabe or Ellie. We were all going to die anyway. Or, at least, one of us would probably die. Probably me. Hopefully me.

That shouldn't have been as reassuring as it was. I made my way to the barred window and peered out at the guards who were stationed outside. I wondered how many of them worked for Byron and how many of them worked for Jonathan. It seemed to me that they would all talk, so why would no one have reported to Byron about what was going on? Did Byron just have a false sense of security living here? And if that were the case, what was Jonathan doing?

I sighed. I would just have to wait and find out. I hated waiting. I was never good at it. Perhaps that's why I could never stick to one town. That and because I always pissed off the wrong person for one reason or another. Usually it was because the person who hired me for sex was in a relationship with someone who had wealth or power and they would blame me for their partner's infidelity. It wasn't my fault they were looking elsewhere for pleasure. Did those people just expect their partner to stay and smile when they didn't listen to them or hear their problems? Listening to someone was bare minimum, and yet it meant so much to so many people.

I couldn't wait to see how Ellie fared against the guards that Jonathan had sent, or I should say how the guards fared against Ellie. She didn't take kindly to people telling her to go with them even when we were younger. I imagined that only got worse over time. Even if they told her everything, she wasn't going to believe it—not with Byron pulling the strings like he was. Speaking of which,

I wondered what Byron was up to. I hadn't heard from him for a few hours, and then he left and came back. Did he know I had left my cell? If that were the case, I felt that he would have come in here and interrogated me. So far, everything had been quiet.

I just had to wait for Ellie and Zach to be brought here. Then I would know the truth of everything going on—or at least that was what Jonathan had said. I didn't understand why he couldn't just tell Gabe and me the plan and then fill in Ellie and Zach later, especially since he took me to see Gabe. Perhaps he just wanted us to feel a false sense of comfort.

Was I being too paranoid? Maybe, but being paranoid is what kept me alive.

There was a knock at the door. I turned to find Byron. Great—that was all I needed.

"Well, Cor, I see you are doing well. You should be thankful to have such nice quarters." Byron smiled as if I were some sort of guest.

I glanced around. I had to admit, this was the nicest cell I had ever been in. But I wasn't going to tell him that.

I turned back to look out the window as I didn't want to see his face. "What do you want now? Didn't you already have your fun at tea?"

He let out a brief laugh. "I suppose I just missed your company. It's not as if I have anyone else to talk to in this place."

I hesitated. Did he tell me about his brother or not? I couldn't remember. I decided not to mention him. "And here I thought you had all the friends. Does no one want to visit for fear they have to talk to you for more than five minutes?"

I caught a glance of his face. His skin turned red, which surprised me. We bantered often, so I never expected to get a rise out of him. "I have plenty of followers. They understand how powerful I am."

"Followers and friends are not the same. That's like saying my clients are my friends. That is definitely not the case."

His face began to regain normal color, and he smiled. "Right, you were a whore. I didn't realize you would stoop so low. I would have given you some money if you had come back to me."

"No, you would have killed me. And prostitution isn't a shameful job. You shouldn't be unkind about the only women who would ever touch you."

The next thing I knew, a fist had hit my mouth. I was really getting under his skin today. I rubbed my jaw.

"Shut up. I didn't come here for you to undermine me. I came to tell you I'm starting the next part of my plan. Your friends better watch where they hide because things are going to get hectic. Don't worry though. I'll make sure you have first-class seats."

With that, he turned and left me in my room. Did he honestly just come in here to boast his plan was going according to schedule? I had expected he was trying to get information out of me, but it was clear he didn't know anything was up.

I turned to the window and stared outside as I rubbed my jaw. He must really not have any friends.

CHAPTER XXII

Zach

So this was Gabe's dad.

He definitely looked like Byron. If it weren't for the fact he appeared a little older and his face was shaped more like Gabe's, I would have thought they were twins. I glanced over at Ellie, who was able to fit in one of the smaller-sized suits that was in the closet. Men's clothes definitely suited her more than women's did. Perhaps I thought that because I had been with her nonstop since we were children. It wasn't as if she grew up wearing dresses either. I mean, maybe every once in a while, but it usually wasn't by choice.

Gabe's dad didn't really seem to care. He glanced at her for a moment, but I couldn't really read his reaction. He was good at hiding his thoughts which, for me, was a giant red flag. It could just come with the territory, but at the same time it made me realize we wouldn't be able to read him or tell if he really wanted to help us or not. Perhaps Ellie would be able to discern what he was thinking —she was a lot better at that than I was.

"Now that both of you are ready, will you join me in the dining room where we can discuss Byron and how to stop him?"

Ellie and I glanced at each other. Ellie was the one to answer. "Won't Byron see us? Or at least find out we are here?"

"Byron and I don't get along, so he won't be coming to this wing anytime soon. He never quite forgave me for having a child with a Sirian. Besides, he's actually going to one of the neighbors for dinner. I expect he won't be back until late."

Ellie asked, "What about his guards? Won't they report something?"

He chuckled. "Don't you worry about that. Now come. I'll send for Gabe and Cor as well."

I saw Ellie's eyes widened. "Cor? Is he all right? Isn't he held captive by Byron?"

Jonathan nodded. "That he is. But I pay Byron's guards a lot more than he does, so they won't say anything about him leaving his cell."

Leading us out into the hallway, Ellie and I exchanged glances. This all sounded rather odd, but we knew our only option was to go for it. It was better than dealing with Byron.

I had been in Byron's grasp for a couple of days before. It wasn't fun. He treated me fine when it came to food and all that, but the things he said were what were really upsetting. He was terrifying to say the least. I never knew someone that dark and twisted. He really didn't care about anyone but himself.

But wouldn't his brother be any different? I assumed he would, but I had assumed incorrectly many times before. He couldn't simply turn us in to his brother, however, and he hadn't done that. So either he was helping us stop him or he something else in mind that I couldn't figure out.

Jonathan led us down the corridors, which must have been the same ones that we had been led up not that long ago. He motioned to one of the men he saw. He appeared like a butler and was a human male with graying hair.

"Can you get my son and the man who is being locked up and bring them to my dining area?"

The man bowed and went off to what I assumed was to accomplish those orders. Jonathan didn't slow down all the way to the dining hall. I was surprised he didn't say anything to Ellie about not wearing the dress, but perhaps Gabe told him how she was, or the guard mentioned how she stabbed him a little. He was lucky to be alive, honestly. Why were they being so sneaky? Was it because they knew we wouldn't believe them and surrounding us would be easiest? They could have tried telling us the truth, although I doubted Ellie would have believed them. I know I wouldn't have.

But how did he know we were in the woods and not back at the hotel? Maybe they tried the hotel first and didn't find us there?

I would ask once we started discussing everything. It seemed to me Jonathan was a businessman, just like his brother. He wanted everything to happen according to his schedule and didn't think about how that would affect anyone else. Normally we wouldn't work with someone like that, unless we really needed cash of course, which was more often than not. However, this was to stop a madman from taking over the world. We had to listen.

We arrived at the dining hall, and it was spectacular. The room was nice too, but the table was covered in all types of food. There was chicken and steak and mashed potatoes and creamed corn. My stomach growled. It had been so long since we had a proper meal. I was going to try my best to not eat like a sloppy, starved man, but I wasn't making any promises. I was going to eat as much as I could just in case we didn't eat again for a long while, just like I should have done in the Sirian Zone. I hadn't gotten a proper meal since then.

"Please sit where you would like." Jonathan gestured to the table.

I didn't care where I sat as long as I got to eat whatever I wanted. I followed Ellie to the far side of the table since Cor and Gabe would still need to be seated once they came in. Two men came over and pulled our chairs out for us.

"Thank you," we both said as we sat down.

I leaned over and whispered to Ellie, "Do you think I can apply for that job? I bet they get paid more than us."

She replied, "Zach, we don't usually even get paid."

"I know. That's why I think it would be perfect. They probably get to eat their share of this in the back."

She smiled but tried not to laugh in case it brought attention or was rude and whatnot. Although there were a few people working in there, none of them said a word. Ellie leaned back over and whispered in my ear.

"I think you would get fired right away for

talking. There's no way you could be that quiet."

She had a point there. "That's true. I talk way too much."

Jonathan took his seat at the head of the table. "We'll start eating once the others arrive. It shouldn't be too long."

I simply nodded as I stared at the food. Were there going to be more people joining us? This was way too much for five people. Perhaps the staff also got to eat with us. If that were the case, then I really should apply for a job here.

After a few minutes, Cor and Gabe entered the room. Jonathan stood up, and Ellie and followed suit. I, of course, smacked my foot on the leg of the table. I bent over a little.

"Ow."

Cor chuckled. "Good to see you two haven't changed."

"It's been what"—Ellie countered—"a day?"

Cor shrugged. "Felt longer."

She gestured around. "You got to stay here, and we had to sleep under the stars and hunt rabbits for dinner. Not to mention our motel is infested with rats and bugs."

Cor turned to Gabe and grabbed his hand. "Oh no, are you all right?"

I held back a smile as Ellie frowned. That was definitely a typical Cor move. Before the conversation could go on, Gabe's father gestured to the table.

"Please sit. After we eat, we can discuss what our plan will be."

Cor and Gabe took a seat—Gabe sitting closest to his father and Cor sitting across from Ellie. She kicked him in the shins. I only knew because I heard him grunt after he sat down. I gave her a thumbs-up.

Jonathan began digging in. "Eat as much as you want. This is all for you four."

And I did just that. My plate was taller than I had ever made at any buffet before. Ellie was giving me judging looks, but I didn't care. I was going to eat it all, so it wasn't like I was wasting food. It was clear we hadn't eaten well in a few days.

Ellie ate slowly, but she was clearly starving. Cor and Gabe didn't eat as much as us. I had a feeling

Byron had fed Cor well even if he was a captive. Byron made sure I ate well when he held me prisoner. If one was suffering from hunger, it was less likely they were going to pay attention to any other way Byron might want to torment him. It made sense to me. Then Gabe probably had afternoon tea or something with his father when he arrived.

Once we finished up dinner and I thought I couldn't eat another bite, the waiters brought in the dessert. There was always room for dessert in my opinion. I shifted in my chair, wondering if that belief was going to cost me. The cake looked too good to pass up though.

"This is a strawberry crème cake," Jonathan commented. "With fresh strawberries from our garden. I hope you all enjoy."

I took my first bite, and I felt as if I were in heaven. The cake was moist, and the cream was fluffy like whipped cream. The strawberries added just a hint of berry flavor. I tried not to drool as I took another bite and another.

After all of us finished our piece, of which none

of us even left a crumb on the plate, Jonathan settled his hands in front of himself.

"Well then, shall we discuss our plan?"

CHAPTER XXIII

Gabe

I didn't know what kind of plan to expect my father to come up with. I doubted it would be anything to hurt his own brother but just something to make him stop, such as capture him, blackmail, and so on. I waited patiently as the waiters filled our drinks with after-dinner tea.

"As I mentioned before, my brother is at an event tonight. He will be staying over there until the next morning. This could be our chance to go through his belongings and find out the truth about what he's doing. Then, from there, we can stop it all," my father explained.

Cor and Ellie tried to speak at the same time. Ellie gestured for Cor to go ahead. He turned to Jonathan. "If you are just looking for evidence, why do you need us here? I mean, couldn't you have one of your many guards go through everything?"

Jonathan smiled. "I can understand how that is confusing to you. However, none of these guards will take action against Byron. Sure, Cor was able to leave his cell, but there would be no way he would be able to leave this building without Byron knowing about it. The guards are careful not to get on either of our bad sides for fear of what would happen."

That made little sense to me. I glanced at Cor, who was still suspicious. There was a lot about my father's life that I didn't know. For example, why he would put up with Byron and let him go visit my mother and I, but never come himself. Supposedly my mother didn't want me to leave the Sirian Zone, which I believed, but I felt that if it were with my own father that she would have let me go. Maybe I was wrong.

That still didn't answer the fact he never visited. Sure, he sent me birthday presents every year, but that wasn't the same. What was so important up on land that he couldn't get away? And why did it seem like it had something to do with this house?

I had always figured I would run into my father when Cor and I were trying to get into the society, but we never did. Come to find out, my father didn't like the society and didn't attend meetings often. Was he just a recluse? Or was he hiding on prupose?

"How do we know you aren't setting us up? Byron does want us all to suffer after all," Ellie said.

Jonathan shrugged. "This would be one strange way to give you over to my brother. I could have just captured you and locked you in a cell. But I didn't." He took a sip of his tea. "I understand why you are cautious, and I get it. I really do. But you have to trust me in order for us to find any evidence of Byron's wrongdoings. He has security defenses and people on the lookout in all his rooms. There would be no way for me to do it all by my lonesome without getting caught."

Ellie glanced at Zach, who in turn glanced at Cor and me. I gave them all a shrug. Apparently they wanted my approval even though I didn't know the man any better than they did.

"What exactly would we be looking for?" Ellie asked. "Does he write stuff digitally or on paper? When we worked with him, he gave us actual papers, but with how much he might be trying to hide his plans, perhaps that isn't the case."

"Although we use technology to keep ourselves safe, we don't use it much in the ways of keeping records. My guess is that he has hard copies if he wrote anything down. I have seen him send out and retrieve letters quite often—he could be talking to someone about his next actions or perhaps setting up his next victim."

"So you want us to look for letters?" Cor asked.

"Yes, and papers and the like. I haven't seen

them in decades, but there were also notes made by grandfather about everything he wanted to happen. They also might be in his possession."

"Well." Ellie began to stand up. "Where exactly is his office?"

Jonathan gestured for her to sit back down. "Not quite that simple. He has multiple rooms, many different safes. It's going to take some time."

"So we need to split up?" Zach asked as he shook his head. "Nothing good ever comes when we split up."

"If you split into two or three groups, it should be fine. I have some maps for you with notes on where to look."

One of the men in the room came to the table and passed out a piece of paper to all of us. I watched Ellie as she simply stared at it.

"Once you all find proof, you can bring it to me and I'll be sure to get it to the right people. Then we'll clean up whatever mess Byron has already made."

"That won't bring back our people though," Cor commented as he folded up the piece of paper.

"Nor will that bring back the woman whom you had a child with. Many people have died. How do you think this will make everything better?"

My father took a long breath and folded his hands in front of himself. "You are right—it's not going to bring any of those people back. But we can stop more people from dying. If we bring out the truth—truth that has proof backing it up—we might be able to convince the others to turn on him."

Ellie peered up from the map. "So pretty much you need us to do the work because if we get caught, your brother already wants us dead, but if you get caught, then you will have to deal with everyone turning on you."

He smiled. "You are a smart one. You sure you don't want to date this one instead, Gabe? Even if she doesn't wear a dress."

Ellie and I made eye contact for a second, then glanced away. When we first met, she was trying to seduce me back to my room so that she could kill me. Cor also looked away since we had a weird love triangle thing going on at the moment.

"She's not my type."

"Right. Well, either way, she's right. Byron is on the hunt for you four, and you pose no risk if you get caught. He'll keep you alive. If it were anyone else, including me, he'll kill them."

"And if we get caught," Zach said, "you'll help us escape?"

My father nodded. "You have my word."

I could tell the others didn't take his word for granted, but I knew he meant it. He had to. It was clear he felt stuck in his position and wanted a way out. He wanted a larger part in my life, but he wasn't able to do or say the right things that manifested that. I knew I could trust him. He was nothing like Byron.

"So, explain the guard situation to me again," Cor said.

"The guards on this side of the estate are under my payroll. As for some of the guards on the other side, I pay them more than my brother when I need something. Not all are in my payroll, however, so there will be people looking for you."

"So if they point their guns or yell at us, they are

on Byron's payroll," Ellie commented. "Great."

"Exactly. You are one smart lass, you know that."

I could tell Ellie wanted to slap him for that comment, but she hid her intentions with a smile.

"So, do any of you have any other questions?" Jonathan asked.

"What time will Byron be back?" Cor asked. "And how many men does he have on his payroll?"

"He has about three dozen on payroll. And he won't be back until morning."

Cor bit his lip but didn't say anything.

"Only three dozen? That's child's play." Zach nervously laughed. "Ellie can take care of that many people in her sleep."

Ellie smiled. "I really could but only if I didn't have to worry about anyone else."

"Speaking of which, how were you able to get Ellie and Zach here?" Cor asked.

Ellie and Zach glanced at each other, then turned to Jonathan. "Yeah," Ellie said. "Care to explain that fiasco?"

"I had a feeling they weren't far behind Gabriel and had my men search the premises. I apparently was correct. I didn't want them to get hurt, so I had them put a bag over their heads. I also didn't want Byron seeing who I was bringing in."

"And Ellie didn't kill all the men? That's impressive."

"I stabbed one of them, but they really took us by surprise. I also had to worry about Zach since they had already grabbed his weapons and had them in their custody while I fought. It was also clear they weren't going to hurt us, so I went with it. Byron's men would have hurt us even if he wanted us alive."

Byron smiled as he sipped his tea. "See, it all ended well. Now, shall we begin this search?"

CHAPTER XXIV

Ellie

I didn't trust him. I didn't trust him at all.

But at least I had my gun and knives back. I placed my hand on my gun, caressing the handle with my thumb. I would not have agreed to anything Jonathan said if he didn't let me have my precious Crazy Jack. He was my pride and joy and was the first gun I ever bought. We had been through a lot together. I wasn't going to use someone else's gun. I was lucky to still have him after everything that had happened.

"You love that gun way too much," Zach commented as we made our way through the corridor. He and I were to search the third floor for rooms that Byron had while Cor went to the second floor and Gabe explored the bottom floor. Jonathan stayed his own study waiting for the outcome of it all.

"Hey, like you weren't happy to have your Lucky Susan back. Besides, I wouldn't have felt comfortable if he hadn't given us some form of weapon—not when there were so many guards working for Byron."

"A lot of them are outside at least and aren't all where we're going," Zach said. "Even if it is strange that there is a bunch of complicated payroll things."

"No kidding. Do you believe all that Jonathan said?"

Zach shook his head. "Not particularly. I think there's more to his plan than he's letting on. However, it's clear he isn't working with Byron, and that's all I care about at the present moment. After this is all over, we can figure out what his intentions are."

I nodded. That's how I felt as well. Byron was definitely the more evil of the two, and Jonathan was helping us get the proof we needed to show the Lyrans, not to mention the rest of the world. However, if the rest were too far gone in all the lies, I had a feeling the Lyrans would be the most likely to listen. So far they had been on the sidelines and watching as everything around them was being destroyed. They would know better than to go along with it. Or at least I hoped.

It wasn't as if I knew anything about politics. All I knew was that people who had power were corrupt more often than not. Everyone I knew who could manipulate the citizens and get them to rebel against whatever they wanted did just that. Krax was one of those people, and he controlled the Silurians with an iron fist. Their culture, however, made that be the only way to rule. If any leader showed weakness, it was used against them, and they soon disappeared from power.

Glancing down at the map, I found that we were Byron's section of the mansion. They appeared to have almost two of everything in this house. Were most mansions like that or did they remodel so that it was practically two houses? I knew that most homes had a lot of rooms for different activities—perhaps it was just that. Did Jonathan have his own section of the clear jail they had at the top of the house or was that all Byron's? I checked the map. It didn't say, but I had a feeling the answer was that it was split. Who would need that many cells? Perhaps their grandfather put them in knowing people would try and stop his plan.

"We're coming up to Byron's wing of the house. Better stay on guard for any men on patrol," I said as I put away the map and pulled out my gun. It was, of course, full of tranks. Bullets were too expensive, and I didn't like killing people if I didn't have to—especially when I knew they weren't choosing to help Byron but more than likely needed the money to survive. The world was a rough one to live in. No, I would save my actual bullets for Byron himself.

As we came up on a corner, I glanced around it. I didn't see any men, but I noticed all the doors were closed. Did that mean they were locked as well? I pulled out some bobby pins to have at the ready.

"Jonathan should have given us a set of keys," Zach whispered.

I shook my head. "He probably doesn't have them for any of Byron's rooms. But he should have brought that up unless he simply assumed they weren't locked."

"Or he took one look at you and figured you could handle it."

I gave him a *ha-ha* look and then as quietly as I could, hurried over to the door. "Watch my back, will ya?"

"Why, what's it going to do?" Zach whispered. I gave him a look, but his attention wasn't on me. He was making sure no one was coming. I kept at the lock and after a few moments was able to unlock the door.

And that was when the alarm turned on. I cursed under my breath. Why hadn't Jonathan mentioned anything about alarms? The more we went along with this mission, the more I was wondering what in the world was going on in Jonathan's head. He seemed smarter than this. Although, I should have been smarter than this as well.

I pulled out my gun and switched out a trank for one bullet and aimed it at the speaker that was blaring the sound. With one hit, the sound stopped.

"Well, shit," I commented as I turned around to find half a dozen guards rushing toward us. I had no idea where they came from, but they were here now.

I quickly jumped behind the desk as bullets came raining down on us. Zach was able to make it behind the sofa. I quickly reloaded my gun with the tranks and peered up at the men. They were bottlenecked at the door, so I only needed to aim in one spot.

Waiting for them to stop firing, I got in position and began shooting. The problem with tranks, other than fact there wasn't blood all over the place, was that you couldn't tell I was firing tranks instead of bullets. These men probably figured I was killing their friends or at least work acquaintances. They opened fire on me again, but since I was taking all their attention, Zach was about to get a few shots in as well.

There were still two left, and they had been able to get in the room—no longer bottlenecked at the door. I could hear them creeping up to the desk I hid behind. I quickly stood up and aimed.

And then I felt a bullet graze my arm. My eyes widened and I cursed under my breath as I shot him in the chest. Zach was able to get the other guy.

"Ellie! Are you okay?" Zach exclaimed as he hurried to me.

I gestured to the door. "Go close it before more come. And lock it."

He nodded and hurried to the door to close and lock it. I sat down the desk and examined my arm. Sure enough, there was a nice hole in the side and blood was pouring out of it. Zach came up to me to check it out.

"Looks like it went all the way through. At least it's your left arm and we don't have to try to get it out."

That was lucky, but I was still injured which

wasn't good. The pain hadn't quite hit since I was still in shock, but I knew it wouldn't be long. "At least the guy had a shitty aim. I was right there. He probably couldn't even hit the side of a barn."

"More than likely he wanted to bring you in for questioning and didn't want to kill you."

"Perhaps. Well, at least I don't have to feel bad for knocking him out. Anyway, help me rip off some cloth so I can bind it up."

"Sure thing."

Zach helped me rip the sleeve off and then tear it into pieces so I could dress it. This was definitely something we had done many times before. It would be a short-term solution, and hopefully Jonathan had a med kit somewhere in this house. I would assume he did. Then I could heal up and be back to my old self again—or, at least, that was what I hoped. Once I was able to wrap it and stop the bleeding, I glanced around at the mess. The guards that littered the floor would wake up in about a half an hour, so we had to work fast.

"Well then, shall we begin searching before these guards wake up and try to kill us?"

CHAPTER XXV

Cor

Something was off about Jonathan, but I couldn't quite place it.

He answered all my questions well enough—I would give him that. But something still felt off. I knew Zach and Ellie noticed it, but this was our only shot at stopping Byron, and we were going to take it.

Did I think it was going to work? Well, to be

honest with myself, I didn't. Byron was a slimy bastard who always seemed to get away. It wasn't fair that evil always seemed to prevail, or at least it had since I had been alive. But we would stop it, however, even if it took our last breath. And I was sure that the others felt the same.

I still couldn't believe that they came back for me. I honestly thought they wouldn't. Perhaps Gabe would have on his own, but I never imagined that Ellie and Zach would. They had no reason to—they had nothing to gain by helping me. They said they had given up taking Byron down, as there was no way we could win against him. But perhaps Gabe talked them into it knowing his father was here.

I had thought it was a long shot getting Jonathan to side with us, but, apparently, I was wrong. That is, if he didn't have something up his sleeve. He clearly wasn't helping Byron, but he could definitely be up to something else. The problem was, I had no idea what it could be.

Or perhaps he really did want to avenge the mother of his child. He hadn't interfered before, but I know if I found out anything happened to Ellie, I would take down that person if it were the last thing I did. Or if someone had hurt Gabe. Well, I guess that was sort of what I was doing with Byron since he had destroyed so many of my friends and family. And because he was downright evil.

As I made my way through the second floor, I noticed that there weren't any guards. Were they just on the fourth floor and outside? Or perhaps Byron took a few with him when he went out.

I pondered on whether Byron going out had anything to do with me saying he had no friends. It probably did, which was just sad. It was no wonder he was so controlling, although that was why he had no friends. And because he was evil, nasty, and a backstabbing sociopath.

Rounding a corner, I stepped into Byron's side of the estate. It didn't seem any different, and if it weren't for the fact I knew where each section of the estate started and ended, I wouldn't have been able to tell the difference. Either this place had been built years ago and had been passed down through the generations, or Byron and his brother had similar styles. I had a feeling it was probably the former, although they did have the same taste in clothes. Gabe also had the same style—specifically the hats.

As I came upon the door to one of Byron's bedrooms, I heard an alarm go off. I quickly hid behind a large statue as guards came running through the hallway toward the stairs. Since it was coming from above me, I deduced it was Ellie and Zach. I could go make sure they were fine and be their backup, but odds were Ellie would be able to take care of it. It also meant there were fewer guards for me to worry about it.

I waited another moment, making sure no one else was coming down the hallway. After I couldn't hear anything, probably because Ellie shot the alarm, I headed toward the door I needed to enter.

According to Jonathan, this was Byron's room. If his office was set up with an alarm like that, then his bedroom was probably the same. I pulled out my knife and felt around to see if I could find some kind of trigger. Sure enough, there was one at the top. I kept my knife sticking out of the top of the door and played with the lock until it clicked open.

I reached up to keep the knife steady and opened the door.

No alarm sounded.

I had found the trigger fine. Now the fun part was to close the door so I could slip my knife out and get to work. Glancing up, I found that there was no trigger. I stared at it for a moment, wondering then why an alarm didn't sound.

Hearing a noise behind me, I spun around and saw there was a maid in the room. She must have turned the alarm off before she began cleaning. I quickly put my knife away and closed the door, giving her a smile.

"Shhh," I said before she could scream. "I'm not going to hurt you. I just need to check out this room."

"But Master Hill wouldn't like that you are in here," she said, her arms shaking. I doubted many people broke into this place… if ever. She probably had heard stories of robbers, though, and thought I was going to hurt her.

"And what he doesn't know can't hurt him. It's all right. I'm a good guy."

"You don't look like a good guy," she whispered as she looked at my clothes and the weapons that Jonathan had given me. She stepped backward to the wall.

I ran my hands through my hair. "Well, you might be right. But I'm good at plenty of things." I stepped closer to her and placed my hand on the wall, leaning in a little. "Care for me to demonstrate?"

She clutched the bedsheet she had been folding before I interrupted her. "I… um… perhaps I should get someone—"

I gently grabbed her chin to look at me. "And kill the mood. Do you really want that?"

Her face was red, but having seduced dozens upon dozens of men and women in the past three years, I had learned to read mannerisms and body language. I, of course, would back off if she said no, but some people need an extra nudge to overcome their shyness. The maid shook her head.

"No, this… this is fine."

I kissed her gently, and she dropped the sheets she was folding. She clutched my vest and pulled me closer. The gentle kiss grew more and more passionate until I could hardly breathe.

After what felt like a couple of minutes of making out, I pulled back. "So do you think you'll keep your mouth shut about seeing me in here?"

She nodded her head and licked her lips. "Yeah, I suppose I could."

"Great. Well, don't mind me as you finish up your work. I'll just be searching around."

I turned to his desk and began flipping through papers. Mainly it seemed like all of them were reminders and notes on what errands he needed to run that day. There was nothing that would be incriminating, even on the dates that he had started the attack against the Silurians. All it said in his notes was that he needed to grab some tea from the local shop.

Pulling out my map again, I made sure I was in Byron's room. According to the map, I was in there. How could he write about such mundane things? I folded the map up again and put it in my pocket.

I opened the drawers to find some nude

magazines, cigars, and a few other things I didn't want to see of his. I didn't care what people did in their spare time, but when it was someone you once saw as a father figure, you just did not want to have those images in your head.

Closing the door, I let out a breath. There was no proof of anything in here. I hoped that the others had found something.

"What are you looking for?" the maid asked as she fluffed one of the pillows.

I had almost forgotten she was in there. I scratched the back of my head. "Oh, papers. Plans. Anything like that."

She bit her lip. "Well, I know where he keeps his most important documents since I do clean up most of his rooms."

I stepped closer to her. "Oh, you do?"

"I don't think I should be telling anyone. Especially strangers like yourself." She bit her lip again as she sat on the bed.

I smiled. So that shyness was just an act. I knew it. I unbuttoned the top couple of buttons of my shirt. "Well, I guess we just will have to get to know each other better."

CHAPTER XXVI

Zach

Why did it feel like we were totally screwed?

Oh, it was because we were. I knew more guards were probably coming our way since the alarm had gone off for a bit before Ellie shot it. Then there was a whole shoot out that I assumed most of the mansion had heard. It was also likely that the cops were on their way if one of the maid or butlers called it in. This was a big mess.

At least Gabe's father could tell the police he didn't need any help, but if Byron got wind of what happened, he would know his brother was up to something and would try and put an end to it all. I was surprised since he was so mad at his brother for not following in their grandfather's footsteps that he didn't try to kill him. Perhaps he did and Jonathan was just that much better than Byron. Or perhaps they didn't turn on family like that. Some people would never hurt their family even if they were in their way. Although, if that were the case, then Byron wouldn't have sent us after Gabe. So maybe Jonathan was just that much cleverer than him.

And if that were the case, then what was his end game?

That would have to be future us's problem. For now, we had to figure out what Byron's next plan was so we could go warn whoever it was he was going to attack, even though we know it is probably going to be the Lyrans. We just needed something tangible to get them to listen to us. But in order to do that, we had to search this entire room as more and more guards headed our way.

I hated staying still like this—waiting for the inevitable. But we had to keep searching the room or else all of this would be for nothing. We had done too much to give up now. What were a couple more people shooting at us?

Ellie seemed fine after getting shot. It wasn't as if bullet wounds were anything new for us. I had been shot half a dozen times and Ellie probably more. We knew how to extract a bullet and bandage pretty well now. We also knew how to stitch up a wound. It was never fun and usually involved a lot of alcohol. If the bullet was anywhere vital, however, we would go in. Luckily none of our injuries had been too serious thus far.

The wound had stopped bleeding but not before leaving blood all over Byron's stuff. Hopefully this wasn't supposed to be a secret mission because, well, it certainly wasn't any longer. I glanced at all the bodies on the floor. It was only a matter of time before they woke up and attacked us again. We had to move, and we had to move fast.

"Find anything?" Ellie asked.

I shook my head. "Nothing. Seems to me Byron didn't want any evidence. Can't blame him—I wouldn't want to get tried for war crimes or treason or whatever."

Ellie grimaced as she moved some books. The arm must be hurting her more than she was letting on. She always did this.

I nodded to her. "Hey, I can look through these piles. Why don't you rest for a moment?"

"No, we need to get through this fast or else we'll be in hot water. I can deal with a little pain. It's not like I'm not used to being in pain."

That was true. I kept on flipping through papers and books and notes to see if I could find anything to help us. So far I hadn't found anything. I let out a sigh.

"Maybe he keeps all his plans in his head. I wouldn't put it past him."

Ellie kept searching, holding her injured arm against her torso. "While I agree he might keep a lot of his plans in his head, I can't believe he would keep everything. I mean, he seems to have some intricate things going on—things that have been going on for generations. There's no way he would want to mess it up by forgetting something important."

She had a point there. I kept on searching for any clues that might help us. So far I had only found history books, maps with no notes on them, classic literature, and so on. None of it had anything to do with the plan that he was trying to fulfill. I rubbed my temples.

"It's not here. All of this is just books he collects. Unless he has hidden notes in all the books, it's got to be somewhere else."

Ellie let out a sigh. "I think you are right. But if that were the case, why would he alarm this place?"

"Maybe he doesn't like other people touching his things. You know how siblings can be."

She snort laughed. "Yeah, I remember when my brother locked me in a closet for stealing his favorite pillow."

I smiled at the memory. Ellie's brother was like a brother to me as well. Although a few years older, he always stood up for me and made sure I was doing all right. Many people in our nation picked on me since I was half human, which was obvious with my red hair. I knew I could dye it, but they all knew who I was—what I was. They didn't consider me to be one of them. They thought I was the reason they lived in a world that hated them.

But Ellie's brother died during the attack. Most everyone did. It was a bitter fact that we kept pushing back in our minds, but it would always be there. Waiting to resurface and distract us. We couldn't be distracted, however, as we needed to bring Byron down once and for all.

"So what do you think Jonathan's intention are actually?" I asked, trying to distract myself from our impending doom.

She shrugged. "I don't know. I think he really wants to help, but as to why now? Perhaps it really was because of what happened to Gabe's mother. If he really cared for her, he would want revenge."

"I still don't get why he couldn't come down here and search. I mean, he could just send his guards to do it."

"I think he doesn't want the guards to go against each other. It would be like a battle, and people who don't need to get hurt will get hurt. I don't know. Rich people always have their own set of rules they play by. And he knows if he makes a move against Byron without having all the information he needs, then it's possible it will move Byron's plan forward."

Ellie had a point there. Byron acted like he would seem like a martyr if we did anything. So Jonathan couldn't make a move on him without it appearing to be some kind of sibling rivalry. Or at least that was what I gathered from it.

"Gabe seems to trust him," I commented.

"Yeah, well, Gabe is a little too trusting of people. You would think after everything that has happened in his life, that wouldn't be the case."

"It's kind of nice, though, that he wears his heart on his sleeve and cares about people even though he grew up the way that he did. Not many would still give a fuck like he does."

She let out a small laugh. "Yeah, I know I sure don't."

I glanced up at her. She didn't seem to be joking. "You are one of the few who are trying to save the world though. You can't say you don't care."

"No, I'm saving the world because I want revenge on Byron and what he has done to us. I'm not exactly doing anything out of the kindest of my heart, not to mention I'm suspicious of every person trying to help us. I shoot first and ask questions later."

When she put it that way, had we really lost our trust in people? I had to agree with her. I wasn't too trusting with anyone new, and I wanted revenge as much as she did—but who didn't? I'm sure Gabe wanted revenge on Byron as well for everything he had done, but I also understood that he wanted to stop this from happening to any other nation. I sighed as I leaned back on one of the statues in the room.

Then it shifted.

I jumped and turned to grab what I thought was an object falling to find that it simply had shifted on purpose. As the statue had moved, so did the bookcase. I started jumping up and down.

"It's a hidden passage! It's a hidden passage! It's a hidden passage!"

Ellie stepped over to examine the bookcase. "Seriously? He's that kind of a villain?"

"Hidden passage! Hidden passage!"

She shook her head. "Are you excited, Zach?"

I nodded. "Yes! This is something you only read about in books! Let's check it out."

Ellie glanced at the men on the ground. One of them started to stir. "Yeah, let's get out of here before they wake up. Hopefully there is a way out on the other side."

CHAPTER XXVII

Gabe

I was… all right with maps. I got around by myself for a while before I met Cor. Luckily this house wasn't a huge nation full of cities and streets. No, it was just a house that seemed to be split in half. Half it was my father's side and half my uncle's. I wondered if their father had the same living arrangement with his brother or if this was something they did after they had their fight. At least it made it easier to search since the sections are clearly labeled on the map. My father and uncle clearly had the same taste in decorations, however. I couldn't even tell when the hallway was changing to lead to Byron's area. Was it all like this from my ancestors decorating or did they do this?

It was much different from the palace I grew up in. I wondered what it would have been like growing up here part of the time. There were a lot less people, even with all the guards. They clearly had guests over every once in a while, but it wasn't like the palace and having dignitaries and guests constantly. If I lived here, I wouldn't have had so many people tell me they hated me. No, I would just have had my uncle telling me that.

Would my father have stood up for me better than my mother had? Or would he have pretended it wasn't happening just like she did? I didn't blame my mother for not wanting to believe that the rest of the people in our zone hated me—no one wanted that for their kid. It was better to believe it wasn't happening. But that made it all the worse, in a way. And I had a feeling, since my father practically abandoned us, he wouldn't have stood up for me either.

I did appear more like a human than Sirian, so perhaps I could have fit in like I had when I was with Cor. Some people knew what I was, but most did not and treated me like any other human. Or, perhaps, no one noticed because I was next to Cor and he was a Kausian. Most typically liked to stare at him and ignore everything else going on.

The only reason some people knew who I was in the society was because of Byron. Once he figured I was trying to get in and prove to him that non-humans, or half-humans, had what it took to stand tall in society, he leaked information about me.

And my father never came to find me.

Perhaps Byron never told him, but I doubted it. My mother was had told him I was on land and Byron was getting the information of my whereabouts somehow. It had to have been through my father, or perhaps Byron simply overheard their conversations. Either way, my father could have come for me in all this time, but he didn't.

So why was he helping us now?

Had I been stupid to trust him? But he was trying to get information on Byron just like we were. He couldn't be doing anything bad—not when he didn't need up to get information that their grandfather clearly gave both of them. No, he was helping us for now and I would just have to keep an eye out ot make sure he wasn't going to try anything else.

I couldn't believe it was actually happening—we were going to take down Byron once and for all. My father loved me and cared enough to want to help us even if it was from the sidelines. At least we had some backing.

Then, after all this was over, I could finally learn more about my father and we could become a family. If it was what he wanted. I wasn't sure he did, but when I found him in the town, he seemed to care. He could have just left me there, but he didn't. Perhaps after this was over, I could hear the truth of why he had kept his distance all these years.

That was something I had always longed for—a family to care for and love. I wanted to be together with Cor and live a normal life. I wanted to have a house and settle down, maybe even adopt a kid. Perhaps Ellie and Zach would be there too, and we could all live together. Then my father could visit, and we would have tea, and everything would be perfect.

Who was I kidding—that wasn't going to happen. There was no way this was going to end well. Byron was always two steps ahead of us. Perhaps he even knew what we were up to and was going to show up and arrest us all. What would he do to my father—his own brother? He made it clear that he felt betrayed by him—so why were they both staying in the same house?

I made my way through the hallway and finally came up to Byron's area. It seemed to me that most of the entertaining was done on the first floor, so it was likely that I wouldn't find anything. But one never knew with Byron. He could have entertained people who were in on the wars he was causing and left some papers there. Or, perhaps, it was somewhere he didn't think anyone would look so that was where he kept everything. I had a feeling we would have to search every nook and cranny of this place in order to find something. Hopefully we would be able to finish before he got back since clearly his guards now knew he was up to something.

Would I run into guards? Would Byron be waiting for me? I knew that was impossible since my father had said he was with a friend tonight. But what there was a trap waiting for us? Or what if there was something even worse waiting for us? These questions filled my mind as I heard alarms go off above me.

My heart was racing at that point. Did one of the others set it off? Who was in trouble? Was it Ellie and Zach or Cor? I knew they could all handle themselves, but I didn't know if I should go help them or not. Wouldn't they help me if I were in trouble? Shouldn't I do the same?

As I debated, I heard footsteps coming in my direction. I quickly moved behind a pillar and watched as two men hurried by. I debated doing anything, but I was lousy with a gun. I just prayed to the goddess that they would be all right.

I turned back toward the rooms I was to search. I

wondered if there were any guards or alarms waiting for me. I gulped as I slowly opened the first door.

No alarm went off. I wished it had as I stared at the person who was sitting in the parlor, smoking on his pipe.

"My dear nephew. I have been waiting for you."

CHAPTER XXVIII

Ellie

Okay, I had to admit, finding a secret passage was really neat.

I had read a few books growing up about secret passages, mainly mystery books. Never did I think people actually had them. We had never encountered any in all our time bounty hunting. Then again, the people we had always been after weren't the richest or cleverest of people. But this

—this was going to lead us to exactly where we needed to go.

Or, at least, I figured I would.

It was a secret passage—it literally had to be leading us to where all his plans were. Why else would there be a secret passage in this place? I mean, it could lead to some sex cult room, which would be a huge disappointment. But more than likely he was hiding the information about his plans in here.

And I would get to rub it in Cor's face that we found it before him.

That part didn't matter, but some reason that excited me. When we were kids, the two of us competed a lot, and clearly that feeling hadn't changed. I wanted more than anything for things to go back to how they were, even though I knew that wasn't possible. Perhaps, deep down, this was how I was dealing with it. Or, perhaps, I was just competitive in nature. Probably a bit of both.

Zach, on the other hand, wasn't competitive but was simply giddy with excitement. He led us up the stairwell, still smiling.

"Hidden passage, hidden passage through the castle. Hidden, hidden, hidden, hidden passage! Oh yeah!" he sang.

I shook my head, trying to hold back my laugh. He made up the most random songs. When all this was over, I was definitely buying him a guitar or something. He would probably have a lot of fun, making up songs and telling tales. I smiled at the thought of a bunch of kids huddled around him as he sang about monsters in the night like some kind of camp leader. Even in Kaus we had camps we could go to when we were kids. Cor and I might have been kicked out one year and never asked to come back. It wasn't our fault so many people were afraid of the large spiders that lived in the desert. And it wasn't our fault we were able to find so many.

Bringing my thoughts back to the present, I focused on the task at hand. Odds were we were going to get our answers soon enough, and I needed to be one hundred percent focused. The pain shooting through my arm made that near impossible. Things were getting a little fuzzy around the edges of my sight. I might have lost more blood than I thought. It was a clean shot, but the cloth I used to cover the wound wasn't quite cutting enough to make the bleeding completely stop. It was already soaked through, and I would need to replace the bandage soon again. Hopefully Jonathan had something I could use once we got back.

I clenched my fist with my good arm and tapped my leg. I would be all right. I had to be all right. Everyone was counting on me, and we were almost done. I could get through this—I had to. I had been through much worse. Much, much worse.

"Hidden passage." Zach kept going with his song, not noticing I was struggling. Either I was better at keeping my head up in times of trouble or he needed to work on his perception skills. Or he was just that distracted about the secret passage. "Something, something, hidden passage."

At least he was entertaining and keeping me focused. Hopefully no one was up ahead who could hear us. With our luck, there was probably an army waiting. At least it would be over quickly, and we wouldn't have to suffer any longer.

Who was I kidding? We would put up a fight and would end up injured and imprisoned and would have to suffer even longer. For someone who said he wanted us dead, he sure liked to play with his victims like a cat tormenting a mouse.

"So what do think we'll find up here?" Zach asked.

"Hmm. I'm not sure. I'm imagining all those books that had the dark passages with candles and skulls. Perhaps even a man playing a piano all creepily." I knew we weren't going to find all that, but I was getting dizzier and was having trouble with coming up anything helpful.

"So am I. Maybe even some treasure of some sort. Like a chest full of stollen gold"

"Why would he have a chest of gold?"

"I don't know—Why would he have a creepy piano?"

That was fair. I was just saying that in scenarios like this, there were ghosts or a creepy villain playing the piano, not that there would be one. I liked reading darker mysteries with ghosts and the like. I hadn't read a book in years, though, as books took up too much space. Perhaps when all of this was over, we could buy a place and have a library. Who was I kidding? We would never have enough money for that, not to mention if we stayed in one spot, it was likely someone would attack us and burn down our house. I didn't want to watch all those books burn. It was heartbreaking.

As we rounded the corner, we came to a small room. It was a bit underwhelming, as I was expecting a huge secret room—especially with how far we walked. I supposed it would be easier to hide a small room than a large room. Stories liked to make everything grand, but this was reality.

I scanned around, making sure there was another way out that we could use as there were a bunch of guards that were going to wake up from the way we came. Sure enough, there was another way out —or, at least, there was another hallway. Hopefully it didn't have an alarm as well, or it didn't lead somewhere with a bunch of guards.

Now that I felt relieved as we had a way to escape, I was able to take a better look at the room.

It wasn't anything fancy. Or at least it didn't look like a place an evil villain used to plot the destruction of the world. It appeared almost like an old attic space with photo albums and diaries. I flipped through one of the diaries.

"Zach, this is…"

Zach nodded as he was holding a different book. "Their grandfather's diaries. Yeah, I saw the dates too. He must have had every step planned for even after he was gone."

"Sick and twisted family, to say the least."

Zach nodded. "At least Gabe didn't end up like them."

I agreed—he was one good thing that came out of his family. He was one of the kindest persons I knew. Their family didn't deserve him.

I grabbed another book to flip through. "Well, let's see if we can find any clues as to what they are going to do next, shall we?"

CHAPTER XXIX

Cor

I buttoned up my shirt as the maid, whose name was Rose, fixed her skirt. Her cheeks were still pink, and she kept a smile on her face.

"Well… that was… worth some information I suppose."

I leaned against the wall and grinned. "I would hope so."

Rose peered at me with her green eyes, then

glanced away. "One day when I was cleaning, I found this." She went over to the wall and moved a statue. Suddenly part of the wall moved. My mouth opened a little.

"A hidden passage?"

She nodded. "I don't think I was ever supposed to find it, and I was too afraid to tell anyone."

That was fair. If someone knew too much, usually they disappeared. She was smart, I would give her that. "So, why are you telling me?"

Rose hesitated for a moment. "I… I know Master Hill isn't a good man. In fact, I know he's a terrible man. I've heard conversations he's had with his colleagues, and I've read the things in there—notes and diaries… I don't want them to happen. It's wrong and needs to be stopped. I promised myself if I ever got the opportunity to help, I would."

I stepped toward the hidden passage and peered up it. I could see a spiral staircase that led up to the next level. It wasn't filled with cobwebs like I would expect, which meant he used it often. By the sounds of it, the notes were up there. Then we could figure out what to do next, and then we could figure out what Jonathan was actually up to.

I wondered if it would lead me to Zach and Ellie, and whether they found the hidden passage. If not, that meant I would win at finding clues first and I could rub it in Ellie's face. She loved it when I did that.

As I studied the secret passage, I asked, "How do I know you aren't going to turn around and alert the guards? I would be trapped."

"There's another way out of the passage, although by the sound of the alarm, you might not want to go out that way. I'll leave this room unalarmed for you so you can get out safely. As for me not turning you in, you will just have to trust me."

I glanced back at her. Her eyes seemed honest enough, but I had been tricked so many times before that I didn't believe I could trust my own intuition any longer. I took a deep breath and let it out slowly. It wouldn't matter if she betrayed us, or if someone else found and arrested us. I knew we were all screwed anyway.

"Right, well, thank you. Hopefully we'll find

something to end this madness. Then you can get a better job—one not under a villainous asshole."

"Thank you. I hope so too."

She smiled and nodded as I turned back and entered the passage. I found the lever to close the hidden door, and it echoed through the chamber.

I felt sweat begin to trickle down my face. Was I really afraid of what I would find? Or was I afraid this was a trap and Byron would be upstairs waiting for me?

The thought of Byron sent shivers down my spine. He couldn't be here—Jonathan said he was with a friend tonight. That made sense since I had provoked him earlier about having friends. So why did I feel like he was going to show up?

Because nothing was this easy—and I couldn't trust Jonathan. Not yet, anyway.

I hated the fact I felt I couldn't trust anyone—not even my closest friends. I honestly didn't think they would come for me—that they had left and had headed for the mountains. I thought they didn't care if I died—that I had deserved it.

Had I been wrong? Did they really care for me

more than that? Why was that a question I needed to ask myself? Gabe had been by my side for two years, and we had been chased after more than once and he always stuck by my side. And Ellie…

I didn't know what to think of Ellie. I had always thought she would be my demise, and now here she was, saving my ass. She was strong and kind—something I could never be.

Well, technically Gabe's father was saving all our asses, but she was coming up with a plan it seemed. It probably wouldn't have worked, and it probably would have ended up with at least one of us injured, but that was our luck.

As I made my way up the stairs, I wondered if they were actually all right. I had heard the alarm earlier, and it was clear that guards went up to see what it was. At least fifteen minutes had passed since then, and I didn't hear any more alarms or notice any more guards. More than likely she was able to take them all out, but then what? Did they just go on with searching, or did they head back to Jonathan? The odds were that they didn't find this passage, so I doubted I would actually run into them.

And there was a part of my mind that worried perhaps they weren't all right—perhaps they had been arrested or, worse, shot and killed.

I shook my head. No, that wasn't possible. Ellie was too good at surviving for anything bad to happen. But what if they had been arrested? Would Jonathan help them? Or would I have to risk my own life to save them? Did I have that in me—to risk my own life for someone else?

I made it to the top of the stairwell and as I entered the room, I came face-to-face with a chair. I quickly lifted my arms, wincing.

"Oh, Cor?" a voice asked.

Now that I wasn't going to be knocked down the stairs, I realized it was Zack. "Zack? Ellie? What are you two doing in here?"

Ellie answered as Zach put down the chair. "I was about to ask you the same question. How did you find this place?"

I didn't want to go into detail as I knew she would roll her eyes at me on how I got the knowledge of this place. "I… uh… found the entrance when searching Byron's bedroom. What about you? What was that alarm I heard?"

"Apparently Byron's office had security, but we're able to take care of them," Ellie explained.

"Not without getting shot though," Zach added.

I turned to him. "You got shot? Not that big of a surprise."

He frowned. "Not me, you idiot. Ellie."

Examining her once more, I noticed the fabric around her arm. Now that I was looking at her closely, I noticed she was a bit pale. She clearly had lost a lot of blood and was trying to act like she was fine. "Are you all right?"

She waved her good hand. "I'm fine." As she said that, she stumbled a little. I caught her.

"You need to rest. Let me take a look at the wound."

"It's just a graze. I'm fine."

"You clearly aren't. Zach, can you look for what we need while I take care of this?"

He stared at me for a moment and then answered, "Sure. I can do that."

I helped Ellie over to the wall and sat her down

so she could lean against it. I knelt down beside her and unwrapped the wound.

It did not look good. She definitely needed stitches, and we didn't have anything with us at the moment. I was sure there was something in this house, but we would have to find it later.

"That bad, huh?" Ellie commented as she watched me examine it.

I shook my head. "It's not the worst I've seen, but you lost a lot of blood and we need to stop the bleeding. I'm going to redress it and hope that will help. You definitely need stitches after we clean it out."

"Which we can do soon. You said there was a bedroom this connected to?"

I nodded. "Yeah, and a bathroom. I'm sure there's stuff in there. And if the maid is still down there, then she can get us a needle and thread."

"A maid? And she didn't alert the guards?"

"Uh… She… um."

She appeared as if she were going to say some not-so-nice words when Zach interrupted us. "Hey, you both need to check this out."

CHAPTER XXX

Zach

I didn't like what I had found.

Byron wasn't alone. There was a whole order of humans that wanted to destroy the other races. Cor helped Ellie up, and they came over to look at the notes I had found. We all stared in silence.

"So there are a dozen people, including Byron, who are in on this," Cor commented.

"Which means even if we take down Byron,

there's still the other eleven to deal with, not to mention they can advance the plan with his death. They can say we're all people from other nations wanting to destroy the humans," I let out a sigh. "This is a mess."

"What do we do then?" Ellie asked.

I shrugged. I really didn't know. Would be able to stop such powerful men? If there were this many with their hands in so many politicians' pockets and have been persuading people for decades, how would we be able to convince the people in general of what was really going on? Even if we showed them these documents, there would be so many people who didn't believe us, and by the time we convinced them, it would be too late.

Ellie answered, "I guess we take this to Jonathan. Maybe he has the resources to solve all this. I mean, it is his brother after all. Then, after he sees these notes and names, he can do something. He's human. The people are more likely to believe him. If we tell anyone this, they'll think we're liars because we are Kausians. But he's a human, and a human with lots of power and, more importantly, money. He'll be able to stop them. Not to mention he has the same amount of power as his brother. He could explain everything and stop this plan once and for all."

"Are we sure of that?" Cor whispered.

The three of us were quiet for a moment. Would that really work? Would Jonathan keep his word and help us? Or was it some kind of ploy and he would eventually betray us?

It wouldn't make sense for him to betray us and join up with his brother. He had plenty of chances to turn us in and capture us, and yet he didn't. There was no way he was in on it all with Byron, but he could stop it with his social status. Or, at least, I hoped.

Ellie broke the silence. "At this point, I think he's our only chance. If not him, then who? Who would listen to three Kausians and a half Sirian? Especially when all of us are wanted for one thing or another even if those allegations are false."

"Except some of them are true," Cor added.

She nodded. "And there's the fact some of the Wanted signs are true. Either way, no one will trust us. If Jonathan can't help us, then I think we have to leave and hide out in the mountains. I don't imagine life will be good for us otherwise."

I couldn't believe what she was saying. Did she want to give up? She wanted to leave this world behind and never look back?

"Ellie…"

"I agree," Cor said. "What point would there be to stay? It would be a death sentence for us if Jonathan isn't able to help. We have a better chance surviving in the mountains even if people say it's impossible. We can shift into Lyrans and keep ourselves warm if need be. No one would be out there to stop us. Harsh conditions isn't anything new for any Kausian."

I wanted to argue with him, but he was right. There would be no point in staying. No one was going to believe us, not to mention they didn't do anything to save our people. After our world was destroyed, no one lent a hand to help us. Why should we help them when we have been surviving on our own all this time?

Ellie nodded. "Fine. It's settled. If we need to

bail, we head to the mountains. We'll need to get supplies from a town and make sure we have enough blankets and coats and food for a while but finally do it. I think with the four of us, it will be more feasible than when Zach and I thought about it before."

We had toyed with the idea of leaving civilization behind, but we never had the money, nor could we keep up having to forge for everything. It was much easier to do that when it wasn't just two people. With four, it would be manageable. With four we would have the manpower and resources. Some of us could hunt, some could build a house, and eventually we would have a place to call home.

I didn't want to live in the mountains, however. It was summer now, so it wouldn't be too cold, but once winter hit… Hopefully by then we would have a house built that could withstand the storms. If not, then we would get to freeze to death. Such fun.

"Shall we gather everything and head to Jonathan?" Ellie asked, then wobbled a little.

"I think we should go down to the bathroom and stitch you up. Then we can figure out what to do next."

I nodded. "Yeah, grab her and let's head down."

I helped Cor balance Ellie and grabbed the notebooks that had all the names and plans that were being carried out. Jonathan would know what to do with them and if he were going to stab us in the back, we would know find out soon enough. As for Ellie, well, we would find help soon and hopefully she would be as good as new. She was one of the strongest fighters I knew, and we needed her at her best, especially if we needed to make a run for it to the mountains. I couldn't imagine if something happened, and we had to venture all the way back to seek help. No, there would be no way that would happen. She would be all right—it was just a bullet wound that didn't hit anywhere critical. She had been through much worse.

But there was a seed of doubt inside of me—a thought of what if something bad were to happen.

CHAPTER XXXI

Gabe

I took a seat across from Byron, my heart pounding in my chest. This couldn't be happening. Why was he here? My father had said he was at a friend's. Did he trick my father? Did he know what we were up to?

"Would you like some tea?" Byron asked as he picked up the teapot.

I shook my head. "No, thank you."

"It's not poison, if that is what you are worried about," he commented as he poured his cup. "I wouldn't do that to my own nephew."

"I find that a little hard to believe."

Byron laughed. "I guess there have been times that I wanted to poison you and see what happens. You see, there are a lot of plants that are fine for humans, but they are not for Sirians. Sometimes they even take hours to take effect."

"Then I'm definitely not going to take a cup of tea from you anytime soon."

Byron didn't say anything but smiled. He stirred his tea and took a sip. "Now tell me, where are your friends? Are they outside trying to break in a save you and your beloved Cornelius?"

I blinked. So he didn't know they were already in the house searching for clues? He only knew I was here snooping around. Did he even know Cor had been taken out of his cell?

"They… are gone. They dropped me off here because I wanted to save Cor, but they weren't for that, so they left."

He laughed. "I don't believe that for a second.

There is no way that Elvira would ever leave her Cornelius to rot in a cell even if it was his fault their people were destroyed."

"No, it was your fault. And she did leave. They made a pact not to come back for each other."

Byron set his cup down and leaned back. "You are a horrible liar, nephew. You always have been. The only person you are good at lying to is yourself. You lie to yourself thinking Cornelius cares about you. You lie thinking you can make a difference in this world. I don't know how you can even live with yourself."

This was how all our conversations had gone since I was a child. I tried to block it out—I tried to tell myself that it was all lies, but there was always a seed of doubt. What if he was right? What if Cor didn't actually want to be with me but just wanted the company? What if now that he had Ellie back in his life, he would leave me?

"I can tell by your face that you know I'm right. You should give up, nephew. There is no chance that you can defeat me. It's not as if anyone is going helping you. Cornelius will leave you for

Elvira. They will live happily ever after and you will be all alone.”

I wanted to tell him he was wrong. I wanted to tell him I had my father on my side—the father Byron swore didn’t love me. I kept my mouth shut, however, and watched as he took another sip of tea.

“How about we bring your father in and he can tell us the truth, hm? He can tell me why he betrayed me. Perhaps with his son here, I’ll learn the truth.”

"Perhaps he actually has a heart, unlike you?"

Byron kept his smile as he took another sip of his tea. "Do you really believe your father has a heart? Do you really believe he cares for you even though he stayed here—held up in his home for your entire life? My brother does not care about anyone except himself. You are the last thing on his mind."

I frowned as Byron motioned to the guard who was standing at the doorway. He nodded, and I presumed he was retrieving my father. The father I thought cared. What if Byron was telling the truth? What if he didn't care? But if that were the case, then why was he helping me now?

I didn't know what to do. I couldn't let Byron know that others were searching for his plans. We needed to succeed in order to stop him. I would act like I was simply here with my father, trying to make a plan against Byron. Since we would be in front of him, he wouldn't go looking for the others.

My stomach began to hurt. It did that when I was nervous. I shifted a little in my seat. I hated it when my stomach was like this, but I was definitely scared—mainly for my friends. Byron was a powerful person, and he didn't care who he stepped on to get what he wanted.

After a few minutes, my father came into the room. Now that I saw both of them together, I saw more of the similarities they had. They both held themselves with authority and had thick blond hair. My father was a little older though and had more wrinkles around his eyes.

My father took a deep breath but then tried to smile as if he were happy to see his brother. "Byron, brother, I thought you were gone this evening."

"Yes, well I decided not to go out. I found out we

had a guest, and I wanted to welcome him. You should have told me my own nephew was visiting. You know how I love visiting him in the Sirian Zone—unlike you."

My father smiled gently. "Well, what can I say? After hearing what happened to the love of my life, I didn't think he would be welcomed by you."

The grin on Byron's lips made me want to kill him right then and there, but I couldn't move. My body was beginning to ache, and I didn't know why.

"Do you have any idea what sort of betrayal I felt when I found out you were with her? When I found out you had a child with her? You went against everything our grandfather ever believed in." Byron slammed his teacup down. I thought it was going to shatter, but it didn't.

My father didn't react to Byron's outburst. "I told you once and I told you a thousand times. I loved her. What our grandfather started was wrong. None of the other nations are out to get us. They are all different and worthy in their own way."

"Lies! They want to bring destruction to our

kind! They find us to be weak!"

"The only thing that is weak is you, my brother. You are so naive and narrow-minded that you can't see the big picture."

Byron stood up and walked over to my father. "Narrow-minded? How dare you!"

"But you are, brother. You think that everything our grandfather put in place was to destroy the other nations. That isn't the case. He put it all in place so we can *rule* all the nations."

My father pulled out a knife and stabbed Byron straight in the stomach. My eyes went wide—not believing what I saw.

"And I'll be the one to rule them all."

CHAPTER XXXII

Ellie

Cor and Zach helped me down the stairs. I did not like feeling weak and having to lean on someone for help. I needed to regain my strength and fast.

I had to admit though, it was nice to have Cor caring for me like this. When we were young and I got sick, he would always come over and make me soup and tend to me. Then he would always end up getting sick after I got better, and I would have to take help him. The memories brought a smile to my face. I missed those days so much. I missed him so much.

But that was a long time ago, and I needed to remember that. We were different people. So much had happened in the past three years. He had a boyfriend—he was no longer my fiancé. I had to move on.

That thought brought pain to my chest. I shouldn't be thinking about our relationship at a time like this. There were people after us, and if we slipped up, we could be killed. I couldn't let that happen—we had to survive this. And if all went to shit, which I believed it would, then we had to get to the mountains.

And then what? Live our days in the wild never to enter civilization ever again? Sure, we could eventually go in and check to see if Byron had succeeded, but if he did, would we get caught? Would they follow us and find out where we were and finally destroy all nonhumans left? I didn't want to think about what the future held. No—I wanted to believe everything would be fine, even though I knew it wouldn't be.

It's not as if I wanted to turn my back on this world, but I needed to think about my own skin. I didn't want to die—I wanted to live and make new memories with my friends. Was that too much to ask for in this world? Just to survive without so much cruelty?

We got to the second level, and Cor opened the hidden passage that went into Byron's bedroom. Inside was a maid cleaning up. I reached for my gun.

Cor grabbed my arm. "No, she's fine." He turned his attention to her. "Rose, do you know where we can find some thread and clean needle?"

The maid turned to us and gasped as she saw me. "Is she all right?"

"She will be once I stitch her up. Can you help?" Cor gave her a cocky smile—the same one he always used when he wanted to get his way. It usually worked. I bit my lip—not wanting to think about what their relationship was. I knew it didn't matter—that was his profession after all. But when we were together, he never looked at any other woman or man. Now he was flirting with everyone we ran into. It made me jealous, and I didn't know how to make that feeling go away.

She quickly nodded. "Yes. I keep a sewing kit in here in case I find any buttons loose on Master Hill's clothing."

The maid hurried and brought out a needle and some thread as Cor sat me in a chair. He turned to Zach.

"Can you search the bathroom for some clean cloths and soap? And bandages."

"Here, let me help you," Rose said as she led him to the bathroom.

I turned my attention to Cor. "Rose, huh?"

He glanced up at my eyes, then went back to my arm. "That's her name."

"And you know this…"

Cor eyed me. "You like to shoot enemies; I like to seduce them. We deal with people differently, all right?"

I frowned a little, but I couldn't argue. He wasn't exactly mine, so it's not like he was cheating on me. "Yeah, well, it would have been a lot of men to seduce upstairs."

He laughed. "That's fair. Although, if you took off all your clothes, I bet you would have caught them by surprise."

If it weren't for the fact my arm hurt, I would have punched him with both my fists. I had to be satisfied with just the one. I hit him and he winced.

"Hey, that was a compliment."

Zach came back with all the materials needed to stitch me up. I peered over at Rose. She was cute, I would give her that. Did Cor think she was cuter than me?

"Byron doesn't happen to have a nice bottle of whiskey in here, does he?" I asked.

She held up his finger. "One moment."

Heading over the nightstand, she opened it and pulled out two bottles. "A twelve year or sixteen year?"

"Sixteen would be great." I smiled. It really didn't matter at the moment, but if I could give him the middle finger by drinking his more expensive scotch, I was going to do it.

She brought over the bottle, and I drank a few

gulps as Cor undressed my arm. I glanced down at it. It was still bleeding. No wonder I was feeling so weak—I was still losing blood.

Cor cleaned it up as carefully and as quickly as possible. I kept drinking, knowing the next part was going to be painful.

"Want something to bite down on?" Cor asked.

I shook my head. "No. Just go for it."

He sighed. "All right. Better look away."

I shut my eyes and grimaced as the needle went into my skin. The wound hurt, but damn the needle made it so much worse. I had hoped the shock and whiskey would have helped, but that wasn't the case. I wanted to chug the whiskey some more, but I needed to stay aware in case more shit came for us.

After a few moments, Cor finally finished up my arm. "All right. All done."

I opened my eyes, and the room felt like it was spinning. Pain was shooting through my arm, but at least the bleeding had lessened. Cor wrapped my arm with some new bandages.

"Do you think you can stand?" Cor asked as he

helped me up.

I wobbled a bit. I was still so weak.

"We only need to get you downstairs to Jonathan. Hop up on my back." Cor turned around and helped me onto his back.

"Excuse me, did you say Jonathan?" Rose asked.

Our attention turned to her. We all nodded as Cor answered, "Yeah, why?"

"Do you mean to say he's helping you?"

Cor nodded again. "Yeah, he's the one who gave us directions. He wants to stop his brother."

Rose fiddled with her hands. "I… I don't know if I would trust him if I were you. I don't have any proof, but there always seemed to be something off about him. I know the two brothers don't get along, but I don't feel Jonathan would do anything like this out of the kindness of his own heart. Just be careful, all right?"

I didn't like where this was going. But what were we going to do? Leave? It's not as if we could get far like this.

Rose opened the doorway and quickly shut it. "There are guards out there. You are going to have to go down the secret passage."

"But we came from the secret passage," Cor said.

Rose shook her head. "You went up, but you can also go down to the first floor. It should be clear. Hurry before they find you."

Cor nodded and Zach led the way. She was right. There were also stairs that led down. We quietly descended to the first floor, and as we reached the hidden entrance, Zach slowly opened the door and we peeked into the room we would be coming out of.

And that was when we witnessed Jonathan stabbing Byron in the chest.

CHAPTER XXXIII

Cor

What in the goddess' name was going on?

My mind was already racing—thinking about what Rose had said about Jonathan. Never did I imagine this was what we would be walking into. The three of us stayed back, waiting to see what Jonathan would do next.

After the shock wore off, I noticed Gabe was also in the room as equally stunned as we were. What had happened while we were searching the rest of the house? Why was Gabe with Byron and his father? And why was Byron home still?

"What do we do?" Zach whispered.

I shook my head. "I don't know. Let's see what he says to Gabe. Maybe this is it—maybe we have finally stopped Byron."

"Or we were set up and Jonathan is going to take over everything," Ellie whispered.

We were all silent, knowing that was a big possibility.

"What are you doing?" Gabe asked his father. "I thought you said we couldn't kill him. I thought you said he would be seen as a martyr?"

Jonathan cleaned off his knife, not even glancing at his son. "That was before your friends showed up. With all of them, I know that they will be able to find my grandfather's plans. You see, Byron was hiding them from me all this time, and I needed them to finish what he started. He also, for the first time in quite a while, he let his guard down. I guess he did have a soft spot for you Gabriel."

"Well fuck." Zach sighed. "Now what are we

going to do?"

I didn't answer. I had no idea. First of all, Ellie was injured, we were quite far from the town to have to carry her, and Gabe was in there with the villain in question. That villain also knew we were somewhere in the house and would have guards searching us soon. Then there was the fact that they had a bunch of guards outside, and they were probably all alerted to keep an eye out for us.

To put it mildly, we were up shit creek.

Gabe shook his head. "That can't be true. You said you were going to help us—you said we would stop Byron and all this madness."

"And I did stop Byron, just like you asked. It is a shame about your mother though. I was hoping to use her to take over the Sirian Zone."

"What… what are you talking about?"

"The reason I seduced your mother—it was to take control and become king, but your zone really hates humans. I think I have a way to win them over, however. Or at least how to win your sister over. Then I can finally take what's mine."

Gabe began coughing. I noticed something dark

in his hand. I felt as if my heart had skipped a beat. It was blood. Why was he coughing up blood? Did Byron poison him? What the heck was going on?

Jonathan went on. "I'll be distraught after hearing what happened to my love and finding out the truth about my brother. He will have poisoned you too, and with your dying breath you will have told me what happened. I'll then have taken revenge and killed Byron. Then I'll go to your sister and explain how I was going to do everything I could to help support her. I'll gain her trust, and, eventually, the people will trust me."

"You will not use her as a puppet!" Gabe stood up. "And you won't get away with—" Gabe started to stumble forward.

Jonathan caught him and started laughing. "Oh, but I will. It seems the poison has already begun to take effect."

It felt as if the world had stopped. What did Jonathan just say? He poisoned Gabe? It wasn't Byron? How could he do that? How could he poison his own son?

We had let our guard down. We had made a

mistake trusting him and now Gabe was going to die. It was all my fault—if I had gotten out of the prison, this wouldn't have happened. If they didn't have to come and rescue me, they would have been all fine. Now Ellie was injured and Gabe was poisoned. They should have left me—they shouldn't have risked their lives like this.

Ellie reached into her back pocket and pulled out her map. I couldn't focus on what she was doing but just stared as I watched Gabe try to stay conscious. My arms and legs began to shake. What were we going to do? How were we going to save him? He couldn't die—not like this.

"There is a stable on the other side of the estate," Ellie whispered. "If we go through those doors and go straight, there is a conservatory that will lead out to the garden. Then after that are the stables. If we can get through those doors, we can find a carriage and get the hell out of here."

"I'm not leaving without Gabe," I said. "We have to help him."

"We'll grab him on the way. But first we need to be very accurate with our aim. If we can take out both the guard and Jonathan, then we'll at least have this room taken care of. Can you two do that?"

Zach and I glanced at each other and nodded.

"Cor, use my gun. It's full of tranks." Ellie reached back and handed me her gun.

I took a deep breath and aimed. "I'll aim for Jonathan. Gabe is a bit in the way, and if anyone is going to accidentally shoot him, it should be me."

"All right," Zach said. "On my mark. One, two, three."

We both shot at our targets and watched as they fell down—immediately affected by the tranks. Gabe hit the ground as well. Not because I shot him, but because the poison had knocked him out.

We rushed out of the hidden passage and went straight to Gabe. I didn't know what to do—I had Ellie on my back, and I couldn't carry him. Should I hand Ellie off to Zach to carry? What would that look like? Would that mean I was choosing one over the other? I wanted to help both, but Ellie was conscious and I didn't know what to do.

"I'll grab him. He will be heavier than Ellie, and

I'm a bit bigger than you, Cor. Keep carrying Ellie," Zack said before I had to make the decision.

I nodded absentmindedly and watched as he lifted Gabe onto his back, and we opened the door to the hallway.

Luckily there was no one there, probably due to them checking the alarm earlier. Zach and I carried the other two across the hallway and into the conservatory. There was no one in there, and we peered out at the gardens.

There were half a dozen guards wandering the area. There was no way we were going to get across without being spotted. I tightened my grip on the gun Ellie gave me.

This was not going to be fun.

CHAPTER XXXIV

Zach

What were we going to do?

There were so many guards between us and the stables. There was no way Cor and I were going to sneak past them all with Ellie and Gabe on our backs. We would get caught right away and probably shot. I doubt they were ordered to take us alive—especially after what Jonathan said about Gabe.

Gabe was still breathing—that much I could tell. But it was slowing down, and we needed to act fast. I couldn't lose a friend like him—not when he hadn't done anything wrong and was one of the nicest people I knew.

Cor broke the silence. "It's pretty dark out there. If we're quiet enough, we shouldn't have a problem getting across."

I turned to Cor. "Are you crazy? There is no way we'll make it."

"Have another idea?" Cor asked.

Ellie joined in the conversation. "It really is our only option. If we stay here, Jonathan will wake up and kill us. We need to get Gabe somewhere so we can try to get him to purge whatever it is he had or make him take some activated charcoal."

She had a point. We needed to help Gabe. I tightened my grip around him. Although I had only known him for over a week, there was no way I was going to let him die like this. I considered him a friend now, and friends stuck together.

I sighed. "Fine, let's do this."

Cor was first to start venturing out into the open.

There were a few trees we could try to run to and gather ourselves. Was it going to help? Probably not.

Cor ran to the first tree, and I followed him. The guards were holding lanterns, but that didn't bring that much light to the area. Most of the light came from the house, and luckily a lot of the rooms on this side were off. Maybe Cor was right—maybe we could sneak past them all.

Peeking around the tree, Cor figured out where next to run. I felt as if I were in some game of hide-and-seek, but instead of simply getting tagged, we would be shot. The stakes had never been higher. Well, except that one time. But I didn't count that.

We set off to the next tree, and none of the guards noticed us. Luckily it was all grass under our feet, so that made our steps practically silent. As for the guards, my guess was that they never had to deal with anyone sneaking in or out before. They were just there as a precaution and because Byron and Jonathan had money to spend.

I couldn't believe what had happened back there. Jonathan had killed Byron and poisoned Gabe.

Why would he do that? Other than because he was a monster.

We should have known better—we should have suspected this. We knew to be wary, but I never could have imagined that this was his intent. And how did he manage to poison Gabe without poisoning the rest of us? He must have laced the food with something that could hurt Sirians only and so the rest of us were fine. If that were the case, then it narrowed it down to a few ingredients. I didn't know any way to counter it though. Medicine was not my specialty.

Byron was dead though, so there was that. The person who had led to our destruction was gone. I didn't feel any different than I had when he was alive. My people were still gone, and it was all because of him. What was the point when we couldn't bring them back? Besides, we still had a big bad that was trying to rule all the nations.

At least Ellie had the notes and books. That would stop Jonathan for a little bit, although I had a feeling many of Byron's colleagues would catch him up. Did Jonathan know who those people were? Hopefully we at least stalled him for a while.

Did it matter though? We were going to hide in the mountains and never look back. Was that still the plan now that we had the books and knowledge of what his plans were? I didn't know the answer to that, and I had a feeling we wouldn't figure that out until we got out of this mess.

I followed Cor to the next tree. The stables weren't much farther now, and I felt as if we were in the clear. We would just have to find a carriage, hook the horses up quietly, and then be on our merry way.

Because that was going to be so easy.

As we approached the stables, I noticed there weren't any guards around. Perhaps this would be easier than I thought. Cor began sliding the door, and it creaked loudly. All of us froze.

"Hey, who's there?" a guard called out.

Spoke too soon.

We hid in the nearby trees as guards approached the stable. Luckily with how dark it was, they didn't see us run off. They opened the stable doors and looked outside.

"We attack them from behind. There are only two of them. We should be able to knock them out without any trouble," Cor whispered.

I nodded as I followed him over. Both of us had our guns at the ready with tranks. We snuck into the stables after them. There were only two, thankfully, and we shot them both before they had a chance to peer behind them.

We grabbed the lanterns. Luckily neither of them broke. We hurried over to one of the carriages and dropped Gabe and Ellie off. Although Ellie was injured, she was able to move to Gabe and check him out.

"He's still breathing, but he's sweating pretty badly. I'll try to wake him and get him to throw up. You two, get the horses ready," Ellie said.

Cor and I nodded and hurried off to get the horses. I moved the two men out of the way for when we stormed out of there. It was only a matter of time before someone else came to check why the other two hadn't left the stables yet.

CHAPTER XXXV

Gabe

A voice was calling my name.

My eyes flickered open to see a face. It was a woman. Mother?

The smell of horses. Hay.

Pain. Coldness.

Something in my throat.

Vomit.

Blackness.

CHAPTER XXXVI

Ellie

I was able to make him vomit, but he passed out again. Hopefully it was enough.

I moved his body so he didn't wake up in too much pain from being in an awkward position. I still felt weak, but I was definitely better.

Cor and Zach were able to get the horses hooked up just as a couple of men entered the stables and began shouting at us.

"You! Stop!"

Zach and Cor hopped on the carriage and used the reins to get the horses going. They didn't seem to care there were men in the way. Both of them jumped out of the way as we came barreling out of the stables.

There were shots fired at us, but they didn't aim for the horses. They knew better than to hurt their own master's horses. Cor guided the horses off the estate. I glanced behind us and found a couple of guards had saddled horses and were running after us.

"Cor, hand me my gun!" I shouted.

He turned and handed it to me. He had to focus on driving the carriage. Zach and I aimed behind us and began firing.

The tranks wouldn't hurt the horses. They would need at least ten or so tranks to have any effect. They would be fine. Besides, Zach and I were great shots. We didn't win shooting competitions for nothing.

I was able to get one straight in the chest. I watched as he fell off his horse and rolled off the road. That was one down—five more to go.

Zach and I were able to knock three more of them, but the last one was giving us trouble. I shot again, and my gun was out of rounds.

"Shit," I mumbled as I patted my clothing. I didn't have any spare tranks on me. "I'm out."

"I have one more," Zach commented as he aimed. He pulled the trigger and shot at the last guard. He went down like the others. We were in the clear—at least for now.

Zach and I sat down and sighed.

"We need to go back to town for our horses," Zach said.

Char and Kevin were still at the stables. I took a deep breath. "Zach… I don't think we can go back for them."

He shook his head. "No, we have to! After everything—"

"We won't be able to take them to the mountains. The terrain is too dangerous. We wouldn't have enough food for them. They would freeze or die. It would be better to take these guys as close as we can and then let them run back here on their own.

This is the closest human town from the mountains. These horses will be fine. But ours… if we let them go, they would have no home to return to. Do you want them to suffer?"

Zach's eyes were sad, but he finally shook his head. "No. You are right. But if we're given the chance, we'll find them, right?"

I nodded. "We will. I promise."

With that, we rode into the night.

CHAPTER XXXVII

Cor

Once we were far enough from the estate, we pulled over to rest and figure out what we were doing next.

We were in the middle of the woods, and it was still dark out, so hopefully no one was tracking us quite yet. Once I stopped the carriage, I turned back and checked on Gabe.

I knew Ellie and Zach were watching him, but I

wanted to examine him for myself. He was still pale but breathing. I didn't know what to do. We couldn't exactly see a doctor, but if we didn't, he could die.

"He's looking a little better," Ellie said. "It's hard to tell in the moonlight and with these lanterns, but his color has come back a little. I made him throw up, so hopefully not much is left in his system."

Zach added. "And he's half human, so he will more than likely be okay. There're a few things that are poisonous to Sirians, so I'm not sure what it was."

His father had poisoned him. I couldn't believe it. After everything Gabe had gone through.

"Should we camp for the night so he can rest? So we can all rest?" Cor asked.

Ellie took a deep sigh. "I don't know. I think we should keep moving and take turns resting. We don't want them to gain on us."

She had a point, but I also wanted to be close to civilization in case we wanted to take him in.

"Cor," Ellie added. "I know you are thinking about taking him to a doctor, but the only thing they can do is make him vomit, which I did. They won't help a bunch of Kausians—especially ones that are wanted. Our best luck of surviving is to keep an eye on him and to keep moving forward."

I took a deep breath. She was right. I turned and snapped the reins.

We couldn't look back.

CHAPTER XXXVIII

Zach

We made it to the edge of the mountain.

Or at least near where there was snow on the ground. Although it was still summer, the snow at this altitude was deep in some spots. The air coming off the mountain was chilly to the bone. Luckily we had a few blankets we'd found in the carriage. We would have to hunt, though, to get some furs. That wasn't anything new to us, however.

We untied the horses and let them run off back toward the home they were from. Horses were quite smart when it came to direction, way more than I was. The sun was beginning to rise, and the sky was a blood red.

What was that saying again about red in the morning?

Gabe still hadn't woken up. He had regained more color though, which was a good sign. We wrapped in him the blankets we had to keep him warm.

Now the next step of our adventure began.

Acknowledgements

I want to say thank you to everyone who made this possible. First off, my husband who "gets the pleasure" of reading all my stories multiple times and has always stayed by my side and pushed me forward.

Also, my parents and family who have supported me since the beginning. To all my friends who get to put up with me talking about my characters, the research I find, and just getting asked the most random questions. Special thank you to my writing group and writing instructors/mentors who have always supported me and believed in me.

A special thanks to my editors at Victory Editing, Mona Finden for this cover WHO DID A FANTASTIC JOB, and a thanks to Biserka Designs for formatting and adding the title.

Lastly, thank you to my readers for supporting me by buying my books. I wouldn't be here without you!

Dani Hoots is a young adult sci-fi and fantasy author that likes to be inspired by ancient tales. She has a background in anthropology, urban planning, herbal science, and sci-fi writing. She enjoys reading about history, astronomy and plants, and in her spare time she is either watching anime, reading manga and books, or drawing. Check out her website for a FREE *City of Kaus* novella!

www.DaniHoots.com

Feel free to email her with any questions you might have!

danihootsauthor@gmail.com